"This is so sudden, Avedon."

"Adrian," he said, gazing into her eyes and squeezing her hands till they ached. "This is not sudden at all. I have wanted to kiss you from the first moment I met you in the village, flashing your dark eyes at me and rattling me off for being a yahoo."

His head inclined to hers. Lucy was aware of a fierce thudding in her breast as the dazzle of his eyes came closer. His hand came to her shoulder. The other stole around her waist, and he pulled her into his arms. She felt the solid, warm wall of his chest pressing against her as his arms tightened. . . .

BABE
AURORA
IMPRUDENT LADY
LACE OF MILADY
VALERIE
THE BLUE DIAMOND
REPRISE
WILES OF A STRANGER
LOVER'S VOWS
RELUCTANT BRIDE
LADY MADELINE'S FOLLY
LOVE BADE ME WELCOME
MIDNIGHT MASQUERADE
ROYAL REVELS
TRUE LADY
BATH BELLES
STRANGE CAPERS
A COUNTRY WOOING
LOVE'S HARBINGER
LETTERS TO A LADY
COUNTRY FLIRT
LARCENOUS LADY
MEMOIRS OF A HOYDEN
SILKEN SECRETS
DRURY LANE DARLING
THE HERMIT'S DAUGHTER
ROYAL SCAMP
LOVE'S QUARREL
MADCAP MISS
THE MERRY MONTH OF MAY
COUSIN CECILIA
WINTER WEDDING
ROMANTIC REBEL

THE WALTZING WIDOW

Joan Smith

FAWCETT CREST • NEW YORK

A Fawcett Crest Book
Published by Ballantine Books
Copyright © 1991 by Joan Smith

Library of Congress Catalog Card Number: 90-93576

ISBN 0-449-21729-9

Manufactured in the United States of America

First Edition: April 1991

Chapter One

Bishop Norris sat with his niece, Miss Lucy Percy, in her aunt's saloon. He was sorry to be the bearer of bad news but relieved that the unsavory affair was settled. "Here is the letter Pewter signed," he said, and handed a paper to her.

Lucy took it and read: "I, Ronald Pewter, agree not to see Miss Percy again in return for a payment of five thousand pounds." The rest of the message was blurred by her unshed tears, but she had read enough. She felt desolate, as if she had been wantonly abandoned by her parents.

She lifted her dark eyes to her uncle and said in a small, disbelieving voice, "So, you were right all along. He was only after my money. I can't believe it."

Bishop Norris took her hands and squeezed them. "I'm afraid that is true, Lucy. Don't spare a tear for him. He isn't worth it."

1

Shock robbed her of emotion. Ronald had seemed so loving, so desperate to marry her, and she had been as eager to have him. And all the time it was only her bank account he loved. Lucy looked numbly around her at the elegantly appointed saloon. Pale rays of twilight filtered through the curtains, picking out the gleam of polished mahogany, the satiny sheen of the striped sofa, and the patina of age on the Persian carpet underfoot. How Ronald had admired this room. The house in Belgrave Square belonged to her aunt, but Lucy had spent the past year there. Ronald, of course, knew it wasn't her house. He also knew it *would* be hers one day.

He knew as well the exact extent of her fortune; sixty thousand pounds. His questions, asked over the period of six weeks, had seemed innocent at the time. "With my estate in Berkshire and your cash—how much did you say it is, love? Ah, yes, sixty thousand. With our combined assets, we shall be quite comfortable. In fact, we ought to buy up the farm adjacent to Wildwood. Is the money in your own control, or must we speak to your guardian about it?"

"I control it outright. I am not a child, Ronald. I am twenty-two years old," she told him proudly. "Papa trusted my common sense."

Lucy stirred herself back to the present. Common sense—she had little enough of that. "Do you mean to tell me he doesn't even own an estate in Berkshire?" she asked, hardly able to credit such treachery from the man she loved.

"Pewter doesn't own the buttons on his shirt. He owes every tradesman in London," Bishop Norris

2

told her firmly. "I am thankful your aunt tipped me the clue he was not quite the thing."

How her aunt's slurs against Ronald had vexed her. Her aunt Percy had been a widow for eons. How should she know anything about love? "I must apologize to Aunt Percy," she said in a humble voice.

"It was your aunt's catching him with his nose in your account book that made up my mind to institute serious inquiries," the bishop continued. Blood suffused the elderly gentleman's pale face as he remembered that letter from Mrs. Percy. Norris's appearance suited the role life had assigned him. He was tall and slender, with kindly blue eyes set in a face that smiled more readily than it frowned. But in a temper, as he was now, he could look fierce.

"I had already ascertained there *is* a family of substance in Berkshire named Pewter, but Ronald is only a distant connection," he continued. "I learned through friends that the heir to Wildwood is a Clarence Pewter. He gave a shocking account of Ronald. You aren't the first lady he's tried his hand at fleecing. It was a similar stunt that ran him out of his home."

Shame, humiliation, and anger mingled with the dregs of grief in Lucy's heart. She felt degraded to have been used so badly. "I don't see why I should pay him a penny!" she said.

Bishop Norris examined her and felt cheered. Her firm chin lifted mutinously. The Percy chin she had. It was going to be all right, then. Lucy always had a deal of spirit. The color was already seeping back into her cheeks, and her eyes were flashing. Such a pretty lass, she would have no trouble finding a proper beau once the fall little season began. She had wasted the spring season on Pewter. Lucy needed a quiet summer away from London, where every street would remind her of her disgrace.

It was a pity her father had sold up Fernbank before his death. That was where she would want to be now. It was her brother's death in the Peninsula two years before that had caused the mischief. Foolishness for an only son, to go joining the army, but try to tell a Percy anything! You might as well shout into the wind. Old Mr. Percy fell ill with grief and was unable to run the place. With only a daughter to inherit, he thought cash would be easier to handle. And perhaps there were too many memories for him ever to be content there again.

Lucy had gone to her aunt Mary Percy in London, and when her period of mourning was up, they decided she should make her debut. Nothing had come of it but grief. The girl took up with Pewter and his set at her first ball and hadn't met anyone worth knowing all season. Never set a toe in Almack's, nor attended the first-rate balls. Fresh from the country, Lucy was too green to be onto the tricks of the world and so heartbroken from the loss of her father and brother that she accepted the first offer that came along.

"You should have consulted me before paying him five thousand pounds, Uncle," Lucy said.

"My dear child, how could *I* pay him five thousand pounds of *your* money without consulting you? I didn't pay him a sou. He was so greedy to get the

4

blunt, he signed the letter and accepted a check. The check was drawn on my account. I had already told the bank not to honor it."

Lucy looked at him in astonishment. "So sly! And you a bishop!" she said in wonder.

"Our mission is to tend our flock," he explained. "To protect the lambs from the wolves. A man can't do that job without having his head screwed on straight. Well, my dear, I have a meeting with some colleagues this evening to prepare the agenda for the archbishop's conference in a week's time, and I must be returning to St. Giles early tomorrow morning, so I shall take my leave of you now. But first I shall have a word with your aunt. You'll be all right, Lucy?"

"I shall get over it," Lucy said. Her trembling lips had firmed to anger, which was only natural. "I'll call Aunt Percy." She left the room. When her aunt went below, Lucy sat dry-eyed and alone in her chamber, reviewing the past weeks in light of her new knowledge. She was beyond tears. Ronald, that handsome paragon, was a scoundrel. Her brilliant future lay in dust and ashes before her.

As she sat, her thoughts turned to the real future. Everyone would be laughing at her. How could she show her face in public? If only she could go back to Fernbank . . . In any case, she wouldn't stay in London. And she would not announce her status as an heiress wherever she went. She would go as an anonymous young gentlewoman of modest means. If ever she loved again, it must be a man whose fortune equaled her own.

Belowstairs the discussion touched on a similar topic to that which occupied Lucy's mind. Mrs. Percy's most outstanding characteristic was common sense. She had never possessed much of beauty, and at fifty years, the last remnants of it were fast fading. She was a thin, gray-haired lady who looked like a dragon and had a heart of cotton wool. It was crushed now, to consider Lucy's sorrow.

"I shall take her away for a holiday," she said to the bishop. "Some place deep in the country, where her story is not known." This was a sacrifice on Mrs. Percy's part, though she would never say so. London was her home, and since removing there upon her marriage to Elmer Percy thirty years before, she had seldom left.

"The talk will be all over town, I daresay," the bishop worried. "There is a pack of hounds like Pewter who will be sniffing after her, trying to learn where she has gone. There aren't many unencumbered fortunes of such a size to be had. You must guard her carefully, Mary, as you did this time, and let me know if trouble arises. By the autumn little season she will be recovered and have another run at finding a husband. It is not easy for you, being saddled with such a responsibility."

Mrs. Percy drew a deep sigh. "Truth to tell, I am fagged to death with all the worry of these past weeks. To see that grinning jackal making up to her, and Lucy not awake to his sort. I wish I could just crawl into a hole somewhere and pretend I am someone else."

A quiet smile hovered on the bishop's lips. "Do it,

then," he said. "Get out of town and change your names. Contact an estate agent, or buy a newspaper. There are always furnished houses to let this time of year. Plenty of families want to go to Brighton, and have to rent to pay the grocer."

"It seems a little irregular," she objected.

"It's an irregular situation."

"I shall discuss it with Lucy."

When the plan was discussed the next morning, it met with Lucy's approval. It was decided that they would remove themselves from London and travel anonymously.

"Let us go as mother and daughter," Lucy suggested. "We'll use an alias—Jones or Smith."

"We will want to keep in touch with friends and business people. It will only cause undue curiosity and talk if we notify them we have changed our names. I think we had best remain who we are and trust to luck."

Lucy drew her brows together in a frown. The idea of a masquerade appealed strongly to her. It lent some excitement to what promised to be a long, dull summer. And it gave her protection from fortune hunters. How could she trust her judgment after this fiasco? "I decided last night that I would pose as a married woman," she mentioned idly.

Mrs. Percy considered it and found the idea had merit. Best of all it relieved her of the heavy task of weeding out suitors. With Lucy there would be suitors, even deep in the country, and even if she posed as a lady of slender means. Had it not been for Ronald Pewter, Lucy could have made a stunning match.

Her eyes were her most outstanding attraction. Long lashes curled away from lustrous dark eyes. Without those eyes, she would be only pretty, but with her lively manner, she would never have been called plain.

"You be Mrs. Percy then, and I shall become a spinster," the aunt suggested. "You can be married to my younger brother, and that will account for our names both being Percy. The mail will bear the right names, and we can sort out the letters between ourselves. I'll have to let the servants in on it, but they are totally trustworthy."

Lucy liked the idea but found a little problem. "How shall I account for being apart from my husband all summer? The Peninsular War is over, so—"

"But Wellesley—the Duke of Wellington now, if you please—is back in the Peninsula in his new role as ambassador to France on some diplomatic mission. We shall say your husband is with him. And to account for the sudden appearance of two ladies in a new neighborhood, we shall say you are suffering from a lung infection, which is why we had to go into the country. You *do* look a trifle peaky, my dear. We shall live simply, keep country hours, go to bed early, and have a nice rustication to get you back in looks for the autumn."

This simple life appealed to Lucy in her present mood, and she agreed. "Let us have a look in the *Observer* and see if we can find a nice quiet cottage somewhere. . . ."

Chapter Two

Lord Avedon was considered quite the eighth wonder of the world in Kent, where he reigned supreme over the neighborhood. This noble paragon customarily spent the season in London, but that spring he had been deterred by the amorous exploits of England's premier fool, his nephew, Tony Carlton. What must the boy do but go imagining himself in love with a highly ineligible widow of thirty years, with two children. Tony was twenty years of age—going on ten, according to his impatient uncle. Lord Avedon was Tony's guardian, and an onerous chore he found it, riding herd on a young buck hot from Oxford. Tony—more formally known as Baron Bigelow—was born to the purple, like his uncle. It seemed a cruel trick of nature to put the brain of a linnet into the head of such a wealthy man. Tony was the owner of impressive estates in two counties.

Tony's mama was Avedon's older sister, and the

estate Tony considered home ran adjacent to Avedon's in a beautiful pocket of country between Canterbury and Ashford. This proximity was a mixed blessing. It threw the mismatched pair together more than was comfortable for either, but it made the chore of guardianship more convenient at least. Bigelow would be coming into his majority in six months, and his uncle held the optimistic hope of inculcating some notion of dignity, thrift, and horse sense into him before that time. On the matter of dignity he was fairly despondent, but of the latter two he had still some hopes. Tony enjoyed a large allowance, more than enough to hold house and tend to his personal needs, but even with five thousand a year, he still pestered his uncle for more.

"I know the income from Fossecourt alone is five thousand," Bigelow whined, "and Fossecourt is the smaller estate."

"You appear to forget Fossecourt is mortgaged," his uncle said curtly.

"Ain't mortgaged to the tune of five thousand," Tony replied. He lounged at his ease in a petit point chair in Avedon's study, his blond curls falling over his forehead and his white hands dangling loosely. He had a somewhat girlish face, white with blue eyes and a petulant mouth. Being a prime *parti*, however, he was invariably called handsome.

His uncle provided a startling contrast. His coal-black hair was severely barbered and as straight as straw. Beneath that jetty cap, a pair of brilliant blue eyes stared from a rugged, swarthy face. Angles of nose, chin, and jaw lent a geometric air to the whole.

Lord Avedon, being even richer than his nephew, was accustomed to hearing his appearance described as "striking." He did not suffer fools gladly, which made it difficult for his nephew.

"The balance goes to pay your gambling debts," Avedon replied. "How you managed to get into the hands of the moneylenders for eight thousand pounds is beyond me, with the size of your allowance."

"Only borrowed five thousand," Tony excused himself. "The rest is interest."

"I hope those two sums tell you something, Tony."

"Yes, they tell me I need an increase in my allowance."

"If you had an atom of brains beneath those guinea curls, they would tell you to stay away from the cent percenters. If you want more income, earn it."

Tony straightened up from his lounging posture and said indignantly, "I hope you don't expect a man in my position to sell turnips from a barrow at the side of the road."

"No, I would expect a cattle raiser to sell milk."

Tony just looked blank. Irony, jokes, insults—they none of them meant much to him. "You're always telling me to be dignified. How can I be dignified with my pockets to let?"

"Oh, dignity! I've given up on that," Avedon scoffed. "To see you dawdle through the village with one of Mrs. Lacey's brats on either hand, dripping ice all over your trousers."

"You can't use that old excuse. Mrs. Lacey's gone away."

11

"Yes, and a good part of your income is gone with her and her brood to Tunbridge Wells, where they belong."

Tony looked infinitely bored. "How can I earn some money, then?" he asked.

"Use your head," Avedon said impatiently. "There are a dozen ways. Keep a sharper eye on your steward. Make better use of your farms. You have a lovely cottage on that little triangle of land where our two properties meet. Rose Cottage has been standing idle these three years since Cousin Hanna died. Bring it into shape and rent it. It would bring five hundred a year easily."

"Pooh, five hundred. What good is that? Cost more than that to fix it up."

"It wouldn't cost five. It only wants cleaning and weeding."

"Anyway, it's half yours. Mean to say, Papa built it on your land. I don't consider it mine in the least. Often wondered why you don't let it."

"Because it is yours, ninnyhammer!" Avedon's patience broke at this lack of interest in important estate matters. "The land was not signed over to your father, but he built the house, and it is yours to do with as you wish. Send Jobber down to clean it up, and rent it."

"You might have told me!" Bigelow said with an injured air. But as the realization that there was money to be had sunk in, he cheered up. "By Jove, I'll do it. I saw the dandiest little curricle-hung rig, Uncle. Yellow, with straw seats and backs. All the crack for summer."

"Grow up, Tony. You have a curricle, a gig, and a whiskey, along with your traveling coach and your town carriage and over two dozen horses. What do you want with another rig?"

"I wager I could get it for a hundred pounds. It's a summer carriage."

"We don't have summer in England," Avedon said comprehensively, though it struck him that he was feeling excessively warm at the moment. "You can console yourself with the thought that the money will help to finance Mrs. Lacey's sojourn at Tunbridge Wells."

"That's small consolation to me. She was a fine-looking woman. Nice red curls." A fond smile hung on Tony's lips.

"And rouged cheeks to go with them, vulgar creature! Next you will be calling her a lady. When you rent Rose Cottage, make demmed sure it is not to a widow with a dozen screaming brats to destroy our peace. The place is nearer to my house than yours. In fact, I shall put the advertisement in the paper myself. We'll advertise in London and hope to get some genteel retired couple."

"Excellent. And about the rattan curricle—"

Avedon speared him with a sharp stare. "If you must have a straw carriage for summer, use the hay wain. Now I'm busy—"

"I'm practically gone."

Avedon said, "Good day," pulled a sheaf of papers toward him, and batted his hand to indicate the meeting was over.

Bigelow unfolded his slender frame from the petit

13

point chair and stalked from the room in a state of high dudgeon. Avedon, glancing in the mirror, thought his nephew strongly resembled an irate rooster.

Left alone, Avedon put his head into his hands and sighed. Beyond the window the trees were in full leaf. It seemed only yesterday he had been looking out at blossoms. How quickly the time flew by. He hadn't really minded missing the season. At one and thirty, he had ceased to find much amusement in it, though he knew he ought to be finding a wife and starting a nursery. His remaining at home had led Lady Beatrice Buckley to hope she might grab him. An unappetizing vision of her spreading girth, invariably robed in outlandish peacock colors, and topped with her black hair arranged in convoluted masses, floated into his mind. He shuddered.

Yet he had no difficulty setting her down when she came calling. A worse outcome of staying at home was that his sister, Sally—Lady Sara to the rest of the world—came pouncing down on him. By some freak of chance, the worldly Lady Sara had married Dr. Rutledge, a minor ecclesiastic. Over the years he had risen to deacon of St. Giles. Archdeacon Nivens had recently died, leaving the way open for promotion. The difficulty was that there were four other deacons of equal eligibility in the running. She wanted Avedon to secure the place for her husband, but Dr. Rutledge was domiciled in Hamphire, where his own connections were restricted.

In any case, everyone knew those appointments

were political. The Tories would choose, and Avedon prided himself on being one of the more liberal Whigs. He didn't know just what Sal expected him to do, but her visit was certainly for the purpose of making him do something. She mentioned a dozen times a day that he should "put in a word," as though his being an earl made him automatically a power in the church.

Lady Beatrice and Lady Sara were only petty annoyances. The real mischief was Tony. The boy was hopeless. Sally hoped to wed him and his estates to her eldest girl, Prissy, but that was a vain hope. A pity he couldn't get Tony married off to someone, but the boy always succumbed to the most ineligible women in the parish.

He'd have to make sure Rose Cottage didn't fall into the hands of some jaded fortune hunter. How would he word the advertisement to weed out that sort? "Secluded country cottage, suitable for retired couple." He jotted down the rent and other details and requested a box number to avoid the use of any name or title. When he was satisfied that he had described a cottage that would suit no one but nuns and octogenarians, he sealed the letter up and directed it to the *London Observer*.

"Here is one that sounds just the thing," Mrs. Percy pointed out to her niece. " 'Secluded country cottage, suitable for retired couple.' It is so difficult to find just what we require. It is in beautiful Kent, quiet location, all conveniences. Servants not provided. That is interesting, for I shall want to take at least some of my servants with me. It is quiet and out of the way, just as we want, love."

"Yes, I'll answer it," Lucy said with no great interest.

As her heart mended over the passing days, she was beginning to wonder if such total retirement would suit her. On the other hand the solicitude of her friends was wearying. Perhaps she would find someone who loved her for herself in Kent. And the best way to insure that was to go as someone other than an heiress. If she met the right man, he would not be too disconcerted to learn she was unmarried and wealthy.

Several other replies to the advertisement were received by Avedon as well. He consulted with his sister regarding which to accept. "Here is one from an officer's wife, Avedon," she said, picking up Lucy's letter. "She is suffering from a lung complaint, poor thing. She would come with her husband's sister— that sounds very respectable. We ought to do what we can for an officer's wife, don't you think?"

Avedon cast a wary glance at his sister. He always suspected any pious utterance from Sally. They were her stock in trade, but at bottom she was moved only by self-interest. Her sweetly smiling face could revert to an expression of sly cunning or mulish obstinacy in the blink of an eye. It had taken him years to figure her out, for she was nearly a decade older than Avedon. She was ostensibly here "to bear him company during his rustication," but he actually

16

saw little of her and would not have complained had he seen even less.

Lady Sally had once passed for a beauty, but as she advanced into motherhood, whatever physical charms she had once possessed had been larded over by weight. She disliked physical activity nearly as much as she disliked to spend a penny or waste one. The pleasure of her life was to advance the welfare of her family. Her two goals that summer were the promotion for her husband and a rich husband for her eldest daughter. Both could be achieved better at her ancestral home than with her husband, so she had torn herself away, to give him peace and quiet for preparing his sermons, while she endured weeks of grinding leisure at Chenely.

"I don't like the sound of a soldier's wife. She might get Tony after her," Avedon objected.

"No, no. She comes with her husband's sister. That precludes any sort of flirtatious behavior, and if she has a lung complaint, she will want the ass's milk that is going to waste every day. Such a shame. When I was at home, Papa always gave me the money from the ass's milk," she added with a sharp shot from her gimlet eyes.

So that was it, Avedon decided. It was the couple of shillings from the ass's milk that had turned Sal into a patriot. "There is one here from a retired vicar and his wife," he mentioned. "They might be company for you."

"Oh, no, Adrian, that is exactly the kind of people I most wish to avoid. They would expect to be invited

17

to Chenely, you know, and you would not like that. They would look for special treatment because I am a clergyman's wife, depend upon it. And the lady with lung trouble will want the ass's milk. We must not forget that. Waste not, want not."

"The decision ought not to hinge on a quart of ass's milk a day," he pointed out with a tolerant smile at her clutch-fisted ways.

"No indeed, but her husband is out defending the country while she is all alone—except for her chaperon. See what a nice genteel hand she writes. Very fine pressed paper, too. She doesn't mention her husband's rank, only that he is an officer. He cannot be a colonel, or she would have said. Perhaps a captain. She might be an elderly woman for all we know. And in any case, with her husband's sister along, there will be no trouble with Tony. She will pay cash in advance—that is a point to consider. The interest on five hundred over the year comes to twenty-five pounds. The vicar mentions terms, you see. They would likely accept a reduction when they find out John is a deacon. Let us accept the officer's wife."

"Very well."

The letter of acceptance was sent out, the Percys' traveling carriage was loaded up, and they were off to Kent to hide themselves in Baron Bigelow's secluded cottage, for Lucy to lick her wounds and throw the neighborhood into a tizzy that would make the Lacey affair look tame in comparison.

Chapter Three

"We will not be so very secluded," Lucy said when the carriage turned in at the proper road. "The last signpost said Canterbury twenty miles, but Ashford is only five."

Mrs. Percy strained her neck out the window to see their new temporary home. In June the garden was at its peak. The flower that give the cottage its name grew in profusion. A tumble of pretty pink roses climbed up the lower brick walls of a half-timbered house. Newly cleaned leaden windows gleamed in the sunlight. The honey-colored oak door caught the rays and shone a welcome.

When the ladies alit, Mrs. Percy's first destination was the garden behind the house. Here she was disappointed. Jobber's hasty refurbishing had not extended to the rear. A tangle of toadflax competed with ivy on the wall that partially surrounded the garden, nearly hiding the stone. She entered the rounded arch and stared in dismay at what had once been a cultivated area.

Mushrooms sprouted amidst the rank grass, and even nettles, those harbingers of wilderness, had established a foothold around the edges. But amidst the jungle her keen eye discerned the bloom of cultivated flowers. The wilted leaves of daffodil and tulip showed where spring's glory had bloomed unseen. Phlox and delphiniums and roses vied with the hardier weeds.

"There is work to be done here," she said with some satisfaction. Bringing order from chaos was a challenge and the very thing to help pass a long summer of isolation. "Look at the rabbits!" she exclaimed as a pair of cottontails stopped and gave her a cool stare.

"And the squirrels," Lucy added. "The place is a regular jungle." She lifted her eyes and beheld in the distance a soaring mass of gray stone. Chenely was built on a prominence that overlooked Avedon's domain. "That must be a noble house," she mentioned to her aunt. "Perhaps there will be balls. . . ."

Mrs. Percy disliked the interest in Lucy's voice and spoke on to distract her. "Are those ravens on the battlements? It reminds one of the Tower of London." As she spoke, a large black bird took wind and soared down from its perch. "Let us go and see if the key is in the door, as the letter said." She had not been able to make out the signature on the letter, for the very good reason that Avedon had made it illegible.

They returned to the front of the house, where the

servants had already opened the door and were busy taking in the luggage. For the next half hour the ladies wandered from room to room, admiring and disparaging various features. The furnishings were respectable without being distinguished. They both liked the saloon, which was made cozy by the sparkling leaded windows, and both found the bedroom walls slanted a little more than was comfortable.

On the day appointed for the arrival of the ladies, Lord Bigelow was at Chenely. Still hoping to cajole his uncle into relenting on the rattan curricle, he was on his best behavior. He offered to drive down to Rose Cottage to see if there was anything the ladies required. Lady Sara was the only one of the family with any real interest in seeing the tenants, but she stood too high on her dignity as an earl's daughter and deacon's wife to call on a mere officer's family— at least until she heard an account of them.

"Take note of what sort of carriage they drive, Tony. See how many servants they bring, and how they dress, and so on," she ordered.

"Dash it, Sal, I can't remember all that stuff. I'll tell you whether they're pretty."

Avedon scowled and ran a hand over his close-cropped hair. "You'd best go with him, Sal. He won't give us a notion what they're like. I hope it wasn't a mistake to rent Rose Cottage."

"It was a mistake for me," Tony complained. "I didn't get to see a groat of the five hundred."

"You will if the ladies like the cottage," Avedon said. "I won't cash their check till they've looked the place over and seen if it suits."

"They will consider themselves on calling terms if *I* go," Lady Sara pointed out.

"You will soon disabuse them of that idea if you wish," her brother parried. "Let us not prejudge them. They may be perfectly respectable, in which case you will enjoy their company."

"I could mention the ass's milk," Lady Sara said consideringly, half looking for an excuse to go. "We might provide them with butter and eggs and greens, too," she added. Her brother gave her a knowing look. She did not consider it pilfering to pocket the gains of these transactions. "The servants take what is left over out the back door, and you do not keep an eye on them as you should, Adrian," she scolded. "What you need is a sharp wife. Lady Beatrice was saying just the other day—"

"I have no need of a sharp wife with *you* in the house, Sal." This leveler was received with a satisfied smile. Lady Sara took no offense at being termed sharp. She was proud of her wits.

"I'll go, then, just to please you," she decided, and went off to get her cherry-trimmed bonnet, to impress the tenants.

Lady Sara never went more than ten yards on foot. For a jog a half a mile down the lane she required the full dignity of her brother's crested carriage and a liveried footman, besides the groom. Tony spurned such an antiquated form of travel and galloped across the meadow on his high-bred mount. He was already seated in the parlor of Rose Cottage when Lady Sara arrived, making himself very agreeable when he discovered his new tenant to be a ravishing young lady with chestnut-brown hair done up in the first style of fashion.

It was not her flashing brown eyes that struck Lady Sara, but the fashionable gown of finest lawn muslin, whose price she pegged to within a shilling. Her practiced eye also cast a glance on a mountain of expensive luggage and the number of servants scampering about. She had already remarked the well-sprung carriage standing in the driveway. She entered with a smile on her wide face, and her hand, encased in lemon kid, extended to greet the tentatively acceptable tenants.

"I am Lady Sara, dear Lord Bigelow's auntie, come to make you welcome. I hope you find everything to your satisfaction?"

As Tony had seen fit to introduce himself as Bigelow, Lucy had to adjust her opinion of the lank gentleman who stood before her. That she had wandered into a hive of nobility had not entered her head till that very moment. Her affair with Pewter had kept her removed from higher society during her one season, and she began to feel a little out of her depth. She said what she felt to be correct, introduced her husband's sister, Miss Percy, and sat down. "I am sorry we cannot offer you some refreshment, Lady Sara, but as you can see, we just arrived five minutes ago."

"It is not to be thought of." Lady Sara laughed it away, while her eyes made a darting examination of the room before returning to Lucy. She began to notice at about that moment that the fine lawn gown encased a rather good figure. "Just the veriest dash

23

of a visit, to make you welcome, and let you know if you want anything, Chenely will be closer than dear Tony's place. Chenely is my family home—you may have remarked the stone mansion up on the hill? I am visiting my brother, the Earl of Avedon."

Lucy was confused trying to figure out so many new names and connections. It seemed odd that the nearer neighbor was not her landlord. "Where do you live, Lord Bigelow? she asked.

Lady Sara undertook to answer the question not put to her, as she frequently did when she wished to impress her hearer. "Lord Bigelow lives quite three miles away, at Milhaven. It is the larger of his two estates," she added rather unnecessarily. "He is my elder sister's son. We are all connected hereabouts."

"I see. And you live in the lovely old mansion on the hill, Lady Sara?"

"I was raised at Chenely—the name goes back to our Norman forebears. Something to do with the oak trees in the park, I believe. I was raised there but am presently living with my husband, Deacon Rutledge, in Hampshire." She rattled on with the names and ages of her children.

Lucy's mind was reeling, but she noticed that her chaperon was nodding her head in the corner, getting the whole of it off by heart. Mrs. Percy was the sort of lady who understood such arcane matters as second cousins once removed and would never say relative when she meant connection.

"We were sorry to learn your lungs have been bothering you," Lady Sara continued, playing the gracious lady. "So fortunate for you that we have an ass in milk at Chenely, and no one requires the milk at the moment. We will be happy to let you have it." She realized that this sounded dangerously like a gift, when she meant it was for sale. She rectified it by adding, "In fact, you will perhaps want to purchase your other dairy products and greens from us, too. We have chickens and eggs fresh daily as well. No trouble at all to drop off, for Avedon sends some down to the gatekeeper's wife, not a quarter of a mile out of the way."

"Thank you. You are very kind," Lucy said. "Certainly we will be happy for the milk and greens, though I do not care for ass's milk."

"But my dear, it is the very thing for weak lungs."

"It doesn't agree with me," Lucy said simply. She had never tasted it, but the idea was repulsive.

It was a pity to lose out on the sale of the ass's milk, but with such a quantity of servants to be fed milk and chicken and eggs, Lady Sara looked forward to a good profit.

Lord Bigelow was not happy to have the beauty's attention diverted from himself and said, "Your husband is in the army, I understand, Mrs. Percy?"

"Yes, Captain Percy is in the Peninsula," Lucy replied.

Lady Sara nodded with satisfaction. Then, remembering that no refreshments were to be forthcoming, she rose to take her leave. She had decided to continue the association and said, "I am giving a garden party on Thursday. I hope you and Miss Percy will do me the honor to attend. It begins at two, but we shall be in touch again before that."

"We shall be very happy to come," Lucy agreed. She accompanied her caller to the door, and her eyes widened at the elegant black chaise, with the crest emblazoned on the door.

She was beginning to realize that life in the country had more to offer than peace and quiet. Bigelow could not bear to be apart from the incomparable and followed her to the door. The baron, a mere stripling, was not attractive, but he was a titled gentleman and must have interesting friends. Lucy regretted that she had made herself a wife, and in the twinkling of a bedpost, she killed off her husband and became a widow. A memory of the past brought to mind the necessity for mourning, and she pushed her husband's death back two years, to leave herself free for any merriment the place might offer. The only problem now was to inform her aunt of her changed status, before she made some revealing statement to Lord Bigelow.

No sooner was Lady Sara out the door than Bigelow returned conveniently to the topic of her husband. "What regiment is Captain Percy in?" he inquired.

"My husband was in the Light Dragoons," she said, with a slight drooping of the lips. "He was killed at Salamanca."

In Bigelow's breast joy wrestled with the need for displaying sorrow and won. "Oh, I say, I'm dreadfully sorry." He beamed. "I wouldn't have mentioned it, but Sal said you were a soldier's wife."

They returned, chatting, to the parlor. "No, I am a widow," Lucy replied firmly, with a meaningful

26

stare at her aunt, who glared but did not deny it.

Bigelow's smile stretched to a grin as the full wonder of this state of affairs washed over him. By Jove, a dasher of the first water right on his doorstep. *In his house,* in fact. A million excuses to be calling on her ten times a day. He soon bethought himself of something better than calling on her.

"I say, I've just had an idea," he announced, jumping to his feet. "Come to Milhaven for lunch."

"No, really we could not impose on you," Lucy said politely, but with interest peeping from her eyes.

"But you have no food here. It will take a dog's age for your servants to get to the village and shop and cook you up something."

"We planned to eat at the local inn," Mrs. Percy said.

"You would hate it. The place is full of farmers and cits. Do come home with me. I'd love to have you."

"Your mother will not be expecting us," Lucy demurred, yet the offer did not seem inappropriate. She looked to her aunt for guidance.

"She ain't home," Bigelow said. "She's visiting Cousin Morton, and I shall have to eat my mutton alone if you don't come with me. Dash it, don't make me eat alone." He included the aunt in his eager invitation, and as Lucy saw no reluctance there, she accepted for them both.

Within half an hour of arriving at their new house, the ladies were off again in their traveling carriage for lunch with Lord Bigelow. Milhaven, while not touching Chenely in size and magnificence, was a handsome brick residence surrounded by park land. The meal provided was indifferent, as Bigelow usually took lunch with his uncle during his mother's absence. But it was enjoyable for all that.

He set out to make himself agreeable to the charming young widow and had no little success. Lucy recognized him at once for a fool, but such an amiable one, and so clearly infatuated with her, that the summer promised to be amusing. He would not let them away till he had shown them all over Milhaven, with heavy emphasis on the stables. When they finally left in order to get their own house set to rights before dark, he trotted alongside the carriage with a besotted smile on his face.

After escorting them to their door and promising to see them again very soon, Bigelow took the idea of going to tell his uncle about the mix-up in the tenant's marital status. No worry clouded his simple mind that Adrian would be anything but as delighted as he was himself at the circumstance.

Avedon was out when his sister returned from Rose Cottage, but they met at tea, and he listened with mixed feelings to her account. He was happy to learn the women were respectable. That they were apparently well-to-do was a matter of indifference to him, though it was what impressed Lady Sara. When Mrs. Percy began to emerge in the tale as "so very charming," "really quite youthful," and finally "extremely attractive," his heart sank.

"How did Tony behave himself?" he asked with foreboding.

"Oh, very polite. Distant, you know. The husband

is a captain, by the way, and he must be youngish, which means he *bought* his commission, so there is clearly money in the family somewhere."

"If there were real money, they would not be renting up a little cottage; they'd have an estate to go to."

Lady Sara ignored the comment. "I counted at least six servants, four women and the groom and a footman. Or perhaps he was a butler."

"Living beyond their means," Avedon scoffed. "Are they to take Jinny's milk, by the way?" he asked, wondering if success in that quarter colored his sister's account.

"No, it does not agree with her, but she wants dairy products and vegetables. I daresay she will be happy for some chickens and eggs as well."

"You speak as though there was only one woman."

"The chaperon was there, too. An elderly lady, a respectable dame, certainly. There is nothing to fear there."

It was at this point that Bigelow sauntered in, smiling from ear to ear in a besotted way that announced he was in love. "Oh, God!" Avedon moaned. "I hope you haven't been making up to a married woman all afternoon, Tony!"

"No, to a widow," he answered, "so there is no need to be looking at me in that disparaging way, as if I was a lame nag."

Avedon jumped to his feet. "Is that Lacey creature back here?"

"Lacey?" Bigelow could hardly remember his former love. "No, you sent her to Tunbridge Wells."

29

"What widow has got that imbecilic smirk on your phiz?" Avedon demanded.

"Widow Percy," he replied promptly. "Mrs. Percy ain't married at all. That is to say, she *was* married. The husband's dead. Ain't that a stroke of luck, Uncle?"

Avedon looked in alarm to his sister. "Sal, is this true?"

Lady Sara looked alert but not worried. "It cannot be. She said her husband is a captain. I'm sure that is what she said. And the letter, you recall, said, 'My husband *is* in the Peninsula with Wellington.' Might she have meant he is *buried* in the Peninsula? Oh, dear!"

"That's the way it is," Tony informed them, beaming with pleasure at this fortunate stroke.

"Did you not mention her wearing something pink, Sal?" Avedon inquired. "An odd way for a respectable widow to be dressing."

"She wore a lovely pink lawn gown, which was very inappropriate for travel, now I think of it. Only it is warm today, of course, and that might account for it."

"The husband's been dead for years. She ain't mourning in the least," Tony assured them.

Lady Sara was never slow to find fault and was soon reassessing her first generous opinion of the ladies. "That was a very lively bonnet I saw perched on the stairpost in the hall, now that I think of it," she said. "*Très gai* for a widow. Almost garish, in fact, with a surfeit of primroses."

"Not so garish as that basket of cherries you had on your head," Bigelow objected.

"I am not a widow, dear," Lady Sara pointed out.

Avedon looked from one to the other in consternation. "You have been telling me for the last quarter hour what a stylish dresser she is," he said accusingly to his sister.

"Stylish for a married lady; garish for a widow," she explained.

"Surely you haven't been at Rose Cottage all this time?" Avedon demanded, turning to his nephew. "You left here three hours ago."

"Of course not, Uncle. I ain't a complete flat, you know. I took the ladies to Milhaven for lunch."

The serene smile on Bigelow's face was the last straw. "You damned cawker!" his uncle exploded. "Dragging a fast widow over to Milhaven, and your mama not even there."

"I never got her alone for a minute. Mrs. Percy's chaperon was with us the whole time. A very respectable old dame, dull as ditch water."

Lady Sara rose and put a restraining hand on his arm. "Oh, my dear Anthony, I tremble to think what your dear mama will say." The trouble, of course, was that his dear mama would not say a word. She was as big a fool as her son, and with no papa in the house, the pair of them would be easily fleeced.

"She wouldn't say anything," Bigelow informed them. "There's nothing wrong with Mrs. Percy. She's very nice. They hadn't a bit of food in the cottage. It was the only thing to do. I'm sorry I hadn't thought of it sooner, for Pikey didn't put on much of a spread for us, though she'll do better another time when I've given her warning."

"There will not be another time," Avedon said sternly. "If some loose piece of baggage thinks to snap up a title for herself by coming here, she is very much mistaken."

Bigelow flew to his feet in defense. "Well, if that ain't just like you, Uncle. Getting astride your high horse and you've never so much as cast a glance on her. She's a jolly nice girl. Tell him, Sal. You saw her. She's nothing like Mrs. Lacey, if that's what has you in the boughs."

His aunt disappointed him. "I remarked a certain resemblance, now I come to think of it. Something around the eyes . . ."

Avedon's face turned livid. "She's some kin to Lacey. That wretch sent her sister or cousin here to show me a lesson!"

Bigelow laughed a tinny laugh. "Now do be sensible, Uncle. Mrs. Lacey don't have a sister, and if she did, she wouldn't have nice brown eyes like Mrs. Percy. She'd have blue ones. The two are nothing alike, I promise you."

"She will get her nice brown eyes out of here all the same," Avedon said firmly. "I won't put up with another month like the past one, worrying about you. I haven't cashed her check yet, and I shan't. I'll tell her we've changed our minds."

Lady Sara thought of the six servants and the luggage and the traveling carriage. She remembered the dairy and vegetable produce to be sold, and she weighed the matter carefully. "No, Adrian," she said sadly. "You sent a letter accepting the offer. That constitutes a contract, you must know. She sent the check in good faith, and if you failed to cash it and start collecting your interest, it is in no way her fault. And in any case, she is not so bad. The sister-in-law appeared sensible. Just keep Tony away from her, and we shall rub along well enough. We shan't do more than nod to them."

"And, of course, send down our farm cart every day," Avedon added snidely.

"That is business, dear. They can make nothing of *that*." A troublesome memory of having invited the ladies to her garden party came to pester Lady Sara. But she had also said they would meet before that time. She would take care that they did not meet, to let the ladies know they were being hinted away.

Avedon rarely looked to his family for guidance and did not do so now. He would not cash the check. He would monitor the situation, and if Mrs. Percy proved troublesome, he would dispatch her.

"I don't want you hanging around Rose Cottage, Tony," he said severely. A glance at his nephew's fatuous grin was enough to tell him the words were not even going in one ear and out the other. They were sailing high over his head. "Do you hear me? Not one penny of the five hundred rent do you see if I hear of their being at Milhaven again."

"Of course, Uncle."

Bigelow had already set up a rendezvous for the next morning at Rose Cottage and had every intention of returning that evening on his way home from dinner with Avedon as well. He knew of old that pretending to agree with his uncle was the best way, and he explained calmly, "I was only making them welcome. I have no further occasion to call."

"See that you don't, then," Avedon warned.

A servant appeared at the door with a silver tray. "Oh, they have brought a fresh pot of tea for you, Tony. How nice," Lady Sara exclaimed. Her sharp eyes observed that he had brought fresh cake as well, and she reached for a slice before turning to her brother. "Tell me, Adrian dear, did you happen to mention to Lord Severn that John is interested in that archdeacon's position we were speaking of?"

The subject of the Percys was dropped, and Avedon turned his attention from one troublesome relative to the other. He thought he could be a happy man if it were not for family.

Chapter Four

While the Percy ladies were enjoying lunch at Milhaven, their well-trained servants made all comfortable at home. The ladies' luggage was unpacked, the backhouse boy was sent to the village to order supplies, and they returned to an orderly household. Cook informed them that they might have fish, fowl, or red meat for dinner, for she had stocked them all. The iceman had heard of their arrival and had filled the icehouse for her, which Cook took as a pretty compliment to herself.

Dinner was chosen, and soon Mrs. Percy had steered Lucy out to the derelict garden to begin making plans. "We must hire a couple of local gardeners. We shall want this grass scythed and the rabbits dispatched. I think the greenery on that wall wants thinning. I shall have the toadflax removed but leave the ivy. Or do you like the pink flowers of the toadflax, Lucy?"

"You're the gardener, Auntie. Do as you wish," Lucy said, and strolled on down to the rear of the garden. "Oh, look, there's a pond here, with frogs!" Her aunt hastened forward to see it.

"An artificial pond! This must have been lovely once upon a time."

It was far from lovely now. What could be seen of the water was an indeterminate blackish-green color, so overgrown with lily pads and sedge that it resembled a swamp. The surface was frequently disturbed by frogs. Mrs. Percy was thrilled to have so much to do in the garden. Other treats were discovered as well. A wrought iron table and chairs were completely buried in nettles. They would require a good cleaning and a new coat of paint.

"This will be a lovely spot to sit and read in the afternoons after we have the place tamed," Mrs. Percy said. "I wonder how much of this space is ours? There is no fence at the back, but only that row of thorn bushes. We could put in a vegetable garden, for this land is going to waste."

"It seems a shame not to," Lucy agreed. "Papa planted something in every corner that was not used for grazing. I don't see any cows nearby."

"We passed a lovely herd on our way to Milhaven. That would be Chenely's farm. Lady Sara said all the land hereabouts belongs to her brother."

Lucy's eyes lifted toward the stone mansion on the hill. She was curious to meet Lord Avedon. "The countryside is beautiful for riding," she mentioned. "I should have brought my mount with me from London."

"Send for it," Mrs. Percy suggested. Her sharp eyes had observed the change in Lucy since arriving in Kent. The bloom was returning to her cheeks, and her eyes were losing that dull look. The best way to put Pewter out of her mind was to let her socialize with respectable people. And Bigelow was eminently respectable, even if he was a fribble. "Lord Bigelow will point out where you may ride," she mentioned.

Lucy gave her a laughing look. "Now don't go imagining a match in that quarter, Auntie. He is a mere babe in arms. I hope he does not prove too clinging."

"We'll see a deal of that long drink of water if I know anything. I am curious to meet Lord Avedon. I wonder if he has any younger brothers. . . ."

Lucy gave her a knowing look. "For me to marry, you mean? Let my poor heart recover first," she said, but in no serious way. Her heart, she knew, was already on the mend. It was her wounded pride that still rankled, and Bigelow's attention was a balm to it.

Mrs. Percy immediately dropped the subject. "Lady Sara lives in Hampshire. I was just thinking, Lucy, as her husband is a clergyman, he very likely knows your uncle Norris."

"Possibly, but he cannot know Bishop Norris is any kin to me. Let us not mention it. Uncle knows we are visiting incognito and will not say anything to betray us."

Mrs. Percy rather regretted she could not bring such a prominent relative forward to impress Lady Sara but was soon diverted back to her garden.

Bigelow dropped in that evening after taking dinner with Avedon. Chenely was his second home, and he kept a full set of clothes there. He had changed for dinner, and it was an extremely elegant gentleman who was shown into their parlor at eight-thirty in a black jacket and pantaloons.

"You put us to the blush, sir!" Lucy exclaimed. "We did not change for dinner, as we were dining alone, and the servants are so busy today settling us in."

Bigelow bowed and said, in one of his more foolish utterances, "Clothes may make the man, but they are not necessary for a lady. That is to say—I mean—dash it, Mrs. Percy, you look charming, as usual."

He was shown a chair, and under the chaperon's deft questioning, he was led to reveal all the circumstances of his family. Of the house of Avedon there remained only his mother, Lady Bigelow; Aunt Sally, the deacon's wife; and Uncle Adrian, who had no brothers. This was sad news. No, the earl was not married. A crusty old devil that no one in her right mind would have, if they wanted the truth, and the worst nipcheese in the kingdom.

Lucy envisaged an elderly miser with a hunched back and foul temper. He must be considerably older than Lady Sara.

Lady Sara's daughter, Prissy, was mentioned, along with the fact that she was a great buttertoothed blob of a girl, the dead image of her mama, only even uglier. She would be here with Aunt Sal now if she wasn't needed at home to look after the family. Which was a blessing for him, if they wanted the truth, for Aunt Sal meant to saddle him with the girl. Keeping her out of sight was the best way to hatch a match, which might just give them some idea what an antidote she was. The name Cousin Morton arose often. He was Mama's cousin, a bachelor in very good financial circumstances, and a great fellow. Lucy's interest was piqued till she learned he resided some miles distant.

All this was interesting to hear, but when it was all told, and he began to tell them the same things again, the ladies found their caller wearying. Subtle hints such as yawns proved ineffective in getting Bigelow to vacate his chair. When the ladies' jaws began to ache from yawning, it was necessary for Mrs. Percy to declare herself fagged from the trip, and remind Lucy that she was still recuperating and should not stay up too late.

This did get through to Bigelow, and he leapt to his feet as if he had been prodded with a hot poker. "I am the most selfish beast alive," he apologized. "Just because I have been having the most wonderful evening of my life is no reason to keep you ladies up. I shall pop around tomorrow morning to see if there is anything I can do for you," he warned.

"Oh, no! You need not put yourself to the bother," Lucy said swiftly.

"It will be my pleasure, Mrs. Percy. There's bound to be a leak or a loose window or a door unhinged. The place is falling apart."

"*Now* you tell us, after gouging us five hundred pounds!" she teased.

"By Jove, I'll ask my uncle to cut your rent."

Lucy did not think it wise to disturb the miser and said that was not necessary. As she led him to the door, she said, "What we are concerned about, however, is the extent of the land that goes with the building. Is it only the hundred feet or so within the wall of thorn bushes?"

"Eh?"

"That matted tangle of bushes at the back, all covered with thorns. I assume they are thorn bushes," the chaperon told him.

"I fancy that's the extent of the land."

"As the area beyond is not in use, we thought we might put in a vegetable garden," Mrs. Percy mentioned.

Bigelow, so eager to please in all other areas, failed them here. "I shouldn't, if I were you. That's Avedon's land, you see. My papa built the house, but Avedon wouldn't give up an inch of land if his life depended on it. But there is plenty of room for a vegetable garden in front."

The ladies exchanged a defeated look. He saw he had disappointed them and sought how to redeem himself. "I'll tell you what I will do, is clear away that jumble of bushes for you."

Lucy remembered the jungle in the back, and said, "You might bring your gun with you. The backyard is full of rabbits."

"By Jove!" This was an undertaking much to his liking.

Bigelow rode home in a trance. He had not a doubt in the world that he was truly in love this time, and with such a nice, respectable lady that not even Uncle Adrian could find a fault with her. He sent for his head gardener before he retired and told him to take a couple of lads over to rip the bushes out at Rose Cottage, for the ladies wanted to put in a vegetable garden.

"Which bushes?" the gardener asked in alarm.

"The ones in front. I don't own the land behind."

"You mean the *rose* bushes, milord?" the gardener asked, aghast. "They're the making of the place."

Bigelow scratched his head. He had only half listened to the talk of bushes and thorns. "They can't eat roses, can they? They want fresh vegetables."

"But the cottage would be nothing without the roses. Your Aunt Hanna's roses are famous hereabouts."

"Just thin the cursed things out, then, and leave a patch for carrots and onions or whatever people grow in a vegetable garden." The gardener glared. "Dash it, do as I tell you! It's *my* house, ain't it?"

The ladies were awakened early the next morning by the sound of gunshots and shouts beneath their windows. Lucy concluded that either Bigelow was a wretched shot, or the garden possessed dozens of rabbits. There was no sleeping for the racket, so she dressed and went downstairs, where Mrs. Percy already sat, trying to rouse herself with coffee. It was seven-thirty.

"Bigelow is very prompt," Lucy said apologetically.

"I've heard of country hours, but this is ridiculous!" her aunt replied. The shots and the shouting slowed down as the thinning progressed, till only an occasional crack rent the air. "We ought not to complain. It must be done if I am to have a garden. I'll thank Bigelow and ask him if he would like some coffee."

He was delighted to accept and came tracking mud into the breakfast room. "I fancy that's taken care of the problem." He beamed. "And by now the bushes ought to be in shape as well."

Mrs. Percy frowned. "I did not see anyone out thinning the thorn bushes," she said, surprised.

"They're chopping down those bushes out front where you want your vegetable garden," he said. "I told you the land behind belongs to Avedon. I dare not touch it."

A strangled sound caught in Mrs. Percy's throat. "You're not chopping down the roses!"

"Er—just the thorns."

She darted to the front door and stared in dismay. The bushes had been decimated, some of them uprooted entirely. Bigelow joined her to receive praise for his alacrity in executing this scheme of his own devising. He was so crestfallen when Mrs. Percy scolded him that his lower lip actually trembled. Lucy shook her head and had difficulty controlling her laughter.

"They are Bigelow's roses after all, Auntie, and if he wishes to destroy them, it is his own affair."

"It was the thorn bushes behind the house I complained of," Mrs. Percy explained.

The chopping was brought to a stop, and Lucy said, "Would you like to finish your coffee before you leave, Lord Bigelow?

Indeed he would. He would have been happy to join them for lunch and dinner as well if he could manage it. "Pray do not be so formal with me, Mrs. Percy. It is time you called me Tony."

It was always an effort to remember that this overgrown puppy was a peer of the realm. "Tony" came so easily to the lips that before he left the table, he was Tony to both ladies. He was eager to get on a first-name basis with Lucy, but she did not make him free of her name, and he had enough breeding not to usurp it.

The ladies had some hope he would leave after coffee was taken, but he lunged into the parlor and took up a seat. "I believe there might be a set of skittles in the shed," he said.

"I must go to the village this morning," Lucy said at once, to be rid of him. "Cook and the servants have given me a long list of items they require."

"I'll take you," he offered promptly. "The greatest luck. I was going to hack over, but I drove my curricle instead, hoping I might induce you to drive out this afternoon."

As this scheme at least got him out of her aunt's hair, Lucy agreed. They jaunted off to Ashford in the curricle. She was happy for Bigelow's arms to tote her purchases. Bowls and brushes, a broom, and ten yards of cheapest muslin for dust rags, turpentine and beeswax, candles and lamp oil were piled one on top of the other. When Bigelow was laden to the eyes, they returned to the curricle to stow the wares.

It was at that moment that Lucy spotted a most interesting gentleman coming toward them. A blue jacket of Bath cloth clung to his broad shoulders. From the immaculate cravat at his throat to his well-polished topboots he exuded elegance. This was no simple country squire! She had been in town long enough to recognize the tailoring of Weston. He was tall and dark, almost swarthy, with a frowning countenance that would be handsome if it were more pleasantly arranged. Perhaps it was the sun in his face that caused that frown. She hoped Tony would know him and make her acquainted.

Bigelow did not see his uncle, as a shiny new tin pail obstructed his vision. Avedon recognized his nephew's bucksins and topboots and was not slow to realize that the dasher with him must be the new widow. Making a pack animal of him already in front of half the town! This was worse than Lacey and her brats. His eyes skimmed over a fetching bonnet trimmed with yellow primroses, the same one of which Sal had complained. Beneath the brim he beheld a pair of laughing brown eyes and a pretty face that his anger soon imagined to be bold. The gown today was not pink but a blue mulled muslin that not even a vicar could find fast. That annoyed Avedon, too, that she should try to disguise herself as a decent woman to con his nephew.

He reined in his short temper to prevent giving Tony a blast in public. He stopped abreast of them and said curtly, "You should have brought Jinny along, if you mean to set up as a traveling peddler, Tony."

"Oh, good morning, Uncle," Tony said, peering

around the side of the pail. "Jinny's the ass," he explained to Lucy.

A brush clattered to the ground, striking Avedon's boot as it fell. "And you are the jackass," he exclaimed before he quite knew what he said. His anger was exacerbated as town folks passed, smirking at his nephew, who performed an ungainly ballet in an effort to balance his load.

Bigelow ignored the remark. "I'd like you to meet my new tenant, Uncle. This is Mrs. Percy."

"So I gathered," Avedon said, through stiff lips.

"How do you do." Lucy curtsied. He nodded briefly but said nothing, nor did he try to lighten his frown.

Lucy felt all the discomfort of his ill humor, if the nephew did not, and found herself babbling on to fill the silence. "I found I needed a great many things now that I am settling in." She retrieved the brush and put it in the pail. "Mops and pails, you see, and Tony was kind enough to offer to bring me to the village."

"I've been meaning to speak to you, Uncle," Tony said. "Rose Cottage is a shambles. Mrs. Percy tells me we are gouging her on the rent, and I believe she has a point."

"I was only funning, Tony!" Lucy said, with an admonishing glance.

The bleeding had begun already! And she called him Tony! The casual use of the first name within twenty-four hours added fuel to Avedon's wrath. "The rate has already been established."

"But Lucy hadn't seen the place then."

45

Avedon's eyes skewered her with a look of pure malice. "If Mrs. Percy doesn't like it, she may leave. Meanwhile, madam, do you have no servants who might better be employed as a beast of burden than Lord Bigelow?" he asked stiffly.

How very angry he was! Such a marked difference from his nephew. Lucy found it hard to believe they shared a single drop of blood. "I have several, but as Tony was at the cottage, he insisted," she replied with a helpless shrug.

Every word she uttered sent Avedon higher into the boughs. He ran an eye over her purchases. "You are an early riser," he said stiffly. "You did not accumulate that load in two minutes." He drew out his watch and examined it. "It is now nine-thirty. May I know at what hour you called on Mrs. Percy, Bigelow? You will be giving her an odd notion of your manners."

The scathing eye that raked Lucy told her it was not his nephew's manners that were in question, but her own. Her temper rose at his imperious tone, and she replied hotly, "It is true, I did not realize provincial manners had become so farouche."

Avedon realized that shot was aimed at himself. "We always try to suit ourselves to strangers, to make them feel at home," he riposted.

"One can only wonder what manner of stranger usually finds her way to Ashford!"

He passed a disparaging eye over her toilette and said, "We appear to be on the route to Tunbridge Wells, madam. No doubt you are familiar with the place."

She would *not* come to cuffs with Tony's uncle. He was a bad-natured skint, and she would *not* let him goad her to indiscretion. "Only with its reputation, sir," she said demurely. "I hear the chalybeate springs are very beneficial to the elderly. Do you find it so?"

Avedon was momentarily thrown for a loss by her new act of modesty. Was there a glint of laughter in those bold eyes? As her meaning sank in, he could hardly believe the chit's gall. Calling him an old man! And to make it worse, he could think of no clever reply to set her down. "I would like to see you at Chenely, Bigelow, as soon as you unload that stuff. Good day, ma'am." He lifted his hat and stalked off, the blood pounding in his ears.

Tony shifted his burden, and the pail fell clattering to the cobblestones. "Now what the deuce has got him in a pucker?" he asked.

Lucy recovered the pail and carried it herself. "Is he always so foul-tempered?" she asked.

"Only when he's mad at me—that's most of the time."

"Why is he angry with you now? Has it got something to do with me?" Lucy asked, bewildered.

"Nothing to do with you, my dear. It has to do with money, you see. He's the greatest skint the world has seen since Adam was driven out of Eden. He thinks we should all stick our blunt in the funds like him."

Lucy pondered this and felt that she had fallen into opprobrium because of her escort. "I hope he doesn't think I let you buy all these things!"

47

"That's probably it," Tony said, "but I shall let him know you wouldn't let me pay a sou."

She was sorry to have met Avedon under such adverse circumstances, but then, a man of such unsteady temperament would never be an agreeable friend, so she tried to forget him. They stowed the articles in the curricle and returned to Rose Cottage, where they arrived not ten minutes after Lady Sara's departure.

Chapter Five

It had not been Lady Sara's intention to honor the ladies with a second visit, but she was put in a good mood by the large order for comestibles received from Rose Cottage. Her curiosity was also rampant. Having called so soon after their arrival yesterday, she could not accurately discover in what manner they held house. She was curious to assess their china, their tea, the apparel of their servants, and most of all to get another look at the widow to see whether she was quite the thing after all.

Her chief aim was not achieved, but she greedily stored up the news that Bigelow was off to Ashford with Mrs. Percy. Avedon would be furious. The highest stickler in the world could not have found a fault in the chaperon. Much as Lady Sara disliked to own it, she was impressed with the lady's speech, her Wedgwood china, her bohea tea, and the immaculate attire of her servants. Even the literature displayed on the sofa table was unexceptionable. No naughty Lord Byron assaulted her eyes. It was a collection of Gray's poetry that lay opened, face down, indicating that someone was actually reading it. John was especially fond of *"Elegy Written in a Country Churchyard."* The chaperon expressed every regret at the decimation of the roses, and indeed it sounded exactly like the sort of muddle Tony *would* make of things.

"It was kind of Lord Bigelow to have us to lunch yesterday," Mrs. Percy mentioned. "I would have sent the servants on ahead to take care of the kitchen, but I was shutting up my London residence, and they were fully occupied."

A London residence was carefully noted and its location obtained.

"In Belgrave Square. A sprawling place much too big for me, but it has been in the family for years, and I do not like to part with it." Naturally it was not said that this domicile had been in her husband's family, not her own.

Lady Sara was eager to discuss the widow and went at it by indirection. "Your late brother was somewhat younger than yourself, I take it?" The interesting possibility had occurred to Lady Sara that the young widow might have nabbed an old gentleman from a higher class than herself.

"Twenty years younger."

No luck there. "What a pity! A young man cut down in the prime of life. Where was he killed?"

Mrs. Percy and her niece had not anticipated such close questioning, and had not hammered out all the details. "Ciudad Rodrigo," she said, and made a mental note to tell Lucy so they would not contradict each other.

"I have a neighbor in Hampshire whose son lost an arm there," Lady Sara said, and went on to make a few pious remarks on the evil of war, as befitted a deacon's wife.

Mrs. Percy used it as an excuse to discover exactly what diocese Dr. Rutledge was connected with. "St. Giles," Lady Sara said. "Our bishop is old Norris, a regular antique, but my husband will smarten him up when he—that is to say—the archdeacon's seat is open. I expect Dr. Rutledge will receive the promotion."

Mrs. Percy thought it best to close this subject before Lady Sara said things she might later regret. The visit progressed agreeably. Lady Sara thought, as she drove home in Avedon's crested carriage, that they had been hasty in castigating the newcomers. She had little feminine company at Chenely, virtually none at close range with Tony's mama away. So long as the widow made no effort to nab Tony, the two houses would remain on terms.

The instant she set foot in the door, she was met with a scowling Avedon, who hailed her into his study to hear his news. "I met that jackass of a Tony in the village, serving as packhorse to the widow," he began, and added details of Tony's burden. "What is to be done about her, Sal?" he finished.

"Oh, dear! And I have just been at Rose Cottage for a coze with the husband's sister."

"We agreed to keep our distance from the pair of them!"

"That was a bit previous of us. There were a few things I wished to discover, and really the chaperon seems well-bred. She was reading Gray's *'Elegy,'* and that, you know, indicates breeding."

"Well, the widow is a saucy baggage, and they must both be got rid of at once."

Lady Sara was not to be bulloxed into any decision till she was ready. "I don't see how it can be done. They have rented the cottage for a year."

"She'll have a proposal out of Tony within a week. He's hanging on her apron strings like a demmed puppy. He was there last night, after I ordered him—"

"We could send Tony off to Cousin Morton."

"He'd head straight to Tunbridge Wells if I let him out of my sight. At least I can keep an eye on him here."

"I could send for Prissy" was her next idea.

Avedon mentally compared Prissy and Mrs. Percy and said, "Much good that would do, with the widow on our doorstep. You could take Tony to Hampshire," he suggested.

Lady Sara enjoyed her annual visit home and had no intention of interrupting it. In her heart she knew Bigelow was a lost cause where her Prissy was concerned, so why lumber the family with him for a visit? "No one can handle him as well as you can, Adrian. Isabel is always saying she does not know what she would do without you." This was met with the disbelieving stare it deserved, and Lady Sara changed her tack. "You have a real knack with the boy. Parish work takes up so much of my time at home that Tony would be free to get into mischief. Don't give him the rent money for Rose Cottage. You said you would not if he went back there."

"That's not enough. We must be rid of the ladies," Avedon insisted.

"I don't see how it can be done. And really—"

"She's already trying to get the rent lowered," he said, and instantly won his sister's acquiescence. "To say nothing of that shopping spree. *That* cost him something.

"This is monstrous of her! You must *do* something, Adrian."

"I'll make life so demmed unpleasant for them, they'll jump at the chance to get their five hundred back and go elsewhere."

"How can you do that?" Lady Sara asked.

"Just watch me," he said, and left the room with a diabolical grin on his face.

Avedon had his own affairs to tend to in the afternoon, but immediately after dinner he mounted his horse and rode down to Rose Cottage. The ladies, edging themselves by degrees into country hours, were just rising from the table and were surprised to receive a caller at such an hour.

"Are you sure it is Lord Avedon?" Lucy asked. The butler assured her it was, and she gave a quiet smile. So the ill-natured earl had come to apologize, had he? That was well done of him, but she would not let him off lightly. "Show him into the parlor, Higgs," she said.

Avedon stood looking around the parlor while awaiting their arrival. His eyes darted hither and thither, seeking signs of ill breeding and finding none. A few elegant bibelots that did not come with the cottage had been placed about, giving the place a lived-in air. There was a tambour frame set up by the fireside. That, he assumed, would be the older lady's. A journal and a few books of poetry lay on a table. Freshly cut roses in two vases filled the air with their scent. Much as he wished he could lay the devastation of the roses on the ladies, he knew he could not. They would have no reason to destroy their own garden. That reeked of Tony.

His determination to turn the ladies off did not falter, but he hoped to do it without nastiness. At the sound of footfalls in the hall he turned. In his mind he held a picture of the bold-faced girl from the village. What he beheld now was a very different sight. Lucy had dressed for dinner, but as she expected no company, her gown was simple and modest. Anticipation lent a sparkle to her eyes, and lifted her lips in a tentative smile. She was accompanied by a chaperon of obvious gentility and breeding.

"Good evening, Lord Avedon," Lucy said, and made a graceful curtsey. "Allow me to present my sister-in-law, Miss Percy." He bowed.

The elder lady shook his hand. "I am happy to meet you," she said. "It is kind of you to call and make us welcome." No other possible reason for the visit occurred to her. His sister had done the civil thing that afternoon; now Lord Avedon had come to call. "Please, do sit down."

After the introduction Lucy seated herself on a chair. Avedon and Mrs. Percy occupied the sofa.

"You have got the cottage fixed up very nicely," he said, pitching the comment between the two ladies.

Mrs. Percy mentioned the roses in an apologetic way. "I'm afraid Tony got carried away," she said, with a rueful shake of the head. Avedon's jaw stiffened, and she assumed it was the loss of the roses that accounted for it.

It was the casual "Tony" that annoyed Avedon. What annoyed Lucy was the stiffening of his demeanor. She had an inkling what was bothering him and spoke on to test her theory. "In all other matters Tony has been most helpful," she said. Again the jaw across from her squared to hostility. "You must not think us forward to use his Christian name," she added. "Your nephew asked us to call him Tony."

"Did he indeed? He is sadly apt to fall into intimacy on short acquaintance, I'm afraid. He is still only a boy, just down from Oxford this spring." The penetrating stare that accompanied this speech assessed Lucy's own age. He could find no sign of a wrinkle or rouge on her face. And she was a good deal prettier than he remembered, too.

A few moments' talk about Tony and Lady Sara ensued, at the end of which Mrs. Percy offered refreshments.

Avedon took the opportunity to get on with his business. "This is not really a social visit," he said. "I'm afraid I bring you unpleasant news, ladies. We had not planned to do it this year, but I am tiling these fields around Rose Cottage. The house is built on my land—no doubt Bigelow told you—and it will be necessary for me to cut across your access road.

You will be cut off from the main road. It will be exceedingly inconvenient for you. I realize this location will be uninhabitable during the tiling and am perfectly willing to reimburse your rent money, along with the cost of coming here and relocating."

Mrs. Percy was the first to speak. "Oh, dear! How unfortunate," she exclaimed. The horror of another move occurred to her most forcefully.

Lucy thought for a moment before speaking. She had detected no warmth in Avedon's manner. He said, in so many words, that he was here on business. And his business, it turned out, was to get rid of them. Her vanity was piqued at his lack of interest in her, and now her anger was fanned by his announcement.

"Is it necessary to actually lay tiles across the road?" she asked.

"The water will only accumulate there if I do not," he explained.

"The land hereabouts does not seem excessively moist," Mrs. Percy mentioned. She did not look for any chicanery and was only making an observation.

"This spring has been unusually dry. You must have noticed the land isn't cultivated. Many years, it is a regular marsh," Avedon assured her.

"It won't take more than an afternoon to tile that little stretch across the road," Lucy said. "It is foolish to speak of moving only for that."

Avedon spoke ex cathedra on estate matters. His word was law. He stiffened and said, "It will take longer than one day. I have contracted the job to an outfit from Canterbury. They dig the whole place up first, then come a few days later and lay the tiles. It will take several days."

"They could dig up that one little stretch across the road on the day the tiles come, though," Lucy persisted.

"No, they were very firm about it. It is two different crews of men who do the work, and the digging must all be done before the tiles are put down—because of the runoff," he added vaguely.

Lucy had very little idea what was involved in the job and shrugged in resignation. "It seems we are to be marooned for a few days, Miss Percy," she said to her aunt.

Avedon stared hard at her. "The situation is not clear to you, ma'am. It will be impossible for the cart to get to you with your milk and vegetables, and equally impossible for you to take your carriage to the village. You will be completely stranded, without food."

His every objection served to firm Lucy's decision to remain. "It is fortunate the iceman has filled the icehouse," she said. "We must stock up before the work begins."

"It begins tomorrow."

"Tomorrow! Could you not have told us sooner?"

"It was just arranged this afternoon. There will be a deal of unpleasantness hereabouts the whole summer," Avedon said. "You can imagine the dust and dirt that will be in the air. You wouldn't be able to stick your nose out the door. To say nothing of the neighborhood crawling with a low class of men— very disagreeable for two ladies living alone. You will certainly want to leave. I will be happy to assist you in every way. I will undertake to find you a nice quiet place ten or twenty miles away, and there will be no additional expense in it for you."

Lucy saw her aunt was caving in in the face of so many problems. It only firmed her own decision to remain. "Why did you not tell us this before the place was advertised for hire?" she demanded.

"The job was scheduled for next year, but the men are available now, and they are very hard to get hold of. I must seize the opportunity."

"Well, it is too bad," Lucy said, "but I don't think we shall move just for that. Miss Percy has a great dislike for moving about. A little dust and noise won't bother us unduly for a few days. As to being unprotected, I cannot believe the work crew will be composed entirely of felons. And we have our male servants."

"You forget the inconvenience of not being able to leave the house," Avedon reminded her. "The village will be inaccessible, and no one will be able to call. It will really be most disagreeable. I am exceedingly sorry, but—"

The gleam in his eyes did not look like sorrow, but triumph, and it made Lucy so angry she wanted to strike him. She would not be driven out of her house by this man, not if he set fire to it. "Is there no other place nearby we might stay for the week the work is being done? You cannot have considered the great inconvenience of moving our belongings and half a dozen servants twice within the space of a few days," she said.

"No, there is nowhere. I repeat, I am very sorry."

"There must be half a dozen inns at Ashford," Lucy said. Her voice was becoming thin.

"You will not want the expense of putting half a dozen servants up at an inn for a week."

"You offered to defray the cost," she reminded him.

Avedon had not looked for such strenuous opposition and assumed Tony was the cause. The chit intended to make a set at him. "I meant a reasonable payment," he said stiffly.

"When your plan is so unreasonable, it seems hard for you to offer only reasonable recompense," Lucy retorted angrily. She knew what would vex Avedon more than anything else and resorted to his nephew. "Tony is our landlord. I shall take the matter up with him," she added haughtily.

The word was like a goad to his lordship. "Bigelow is a minor. Don't look for him to foot the bill. I manage all his affairs till he grows up. It is my duty to protect him from being duped."

"You cannot say we are trying to dupe him! It is ourselves who are being duped, coming to a place described as a quiet cottage and learning it is to be turned into a field of dust and mud, with dangerous men lurking about."

"There was no deceit intended, I promise you. I have offered to help you leave. I see you are quite determined to remain. You will realize the generosity of my offer when you are cut off from any travel. I will look forward to hearing from you. You may send a servant to Chenely to notify me when you change your mind." A haughty stare accompanied this piece of studied arrogance. Don't come yourself, in other words. Avedon rose and took his leave, while the stunned ladies looked at each other in disbelief.

"What can be the meaning of this?" Lucy asked her aunt.

"Very odd. I would say he is eager to be rid of us if it were not that the rest of the family are so gracious—Lady Sara coming twice, and Tony all but living here. It is not as though Tony hired us the place without his uncle's sanction. Lord Avedon handles Tony's affairs himself. He wanted to rent it, but once we came, he wants to be rid of us. And I think he will succeed, for I have no desire to be surrounded with shouting workmen and fields of mud. Such a bother!"

"The road is an excuse, not a reason," Lucy said angrily, "and I think I know the reason."

"What do you mean, my dear?"

"Bigelow. He thinks I'm throwing my cap at him."

"I wondered at that crack about being a mere schoolboy and being duped."

"He was mad as a hornet when he saw us together in the village. That is what is at the bottom of this, Auntie, mark my words. As if I cared tuppence for that little—oh, it is too absurd. He must know I am too old for Tony. He looked hard enough at me. And if I *did* marry him, what is wrong in that?"

"Lord Avedon does not know you are Miss Percy, heiress. He believes you to be a captain's widow. He knows nothing of your fortune."

"That is a change!" Lucy said, and laughed at the irony of it. "More and more do I realize Uncle Norris was right. It was the money Pewter was after, and without it, I am wished at Jericho. Most humiliating."

Miss Percy was happy to see how Lucy's spirits

had improved, despite her speech. "There is a little something I meant to discuss with you, Lucy. When Lady Sara was here today, she asked some questions about your 'husband' that I had a little trouble answering. Let us make up a history for him, so that we both tell the same tale."

"Let us use my brother Alex. We are both familiar with his history. In fact, I have already told Tony my husband was killed at Salamanca, like Alex. I think I might have called him Alex, too. That will be the easiest way to keep our stories straight."

"Oh, dear! That is a bit tricky. I told Lady Sara your husband was killed at Ciudad Rodrigo. If the subject arises again, I shall say I meant the province of Salamanca. At least Ciudad Rodrigo is in that province. Not likely it will come up again. Now, about this business of moving, do we let Avedon bounce us off? I can see you have taken him in aversion and dislike to be bested by him."

"If you will agree to it, Auntie, I shall stick it here if our supplies have to be flown in by balloon. And I shall give Lord Avedon a good scare for his impertinence, too. When Tony—*dear* Tony—calls tomorrow morning bright and early, he will be invited to luncheon, and that for milord Avedon." She snapped her fingers and laughed.

Such a bright laugh, just like her old self. Her aunt saw that this little battle was better than a tonic. She wouldn't mind teaching Lord Avedon a lesson herself.

61

Chapter Six

Lord Avedon executed his threat with unholy celerity. When the ladies rose the next morning, they saw a crew of workmen already digging up the road to a depth much greater than the laying of tiles required, and making a deal of noise while they were about it. The air rang with laughter, shouts, and an occasional curse. The road, Lucy noted, was the first thing being dug. The fields on either side of it were also excavated, in case any enterprising carriage had the idea of detouring around the road.

The digging extended, over the morning, in such a wide swath that it met the wild shrubbery growing five or six feet high, and getting a carriage though was impossible. No fresh supplies were brought down from Chenely, but the milk and cream had not curdled yet, so the ladies were not deprived of tea. As the morning progressed, the incessant noise preyed on poor Mrs. Percy's ears to no small degree.

Although she had the windows closed, dust seeped in around the frames, and soon the furnishings wore a coating of brown powder.

When Tony came cantering along in his yellow curricle, he could hardly see Rose Cottage for the dust, and he could not get his carriage in. He retraced his route down the main road and up the sweeping drive to Chenely, to demand of his uncle what was going forth.

Avedon glanced up from his paperwork and said, "I am having tiles laid in my meadow."

"You ain't having tiles laid across the road!" Tony challenged. "And you shouldn't be doing it now, when the Percys have just arrived. What must they think?"

"I gave them advance warning."

"Dash it, Uncle Adrian, that's demmed uncivil. The place is clouded in dust."

"Civility and consideration form no part of my plan," Avedon said blandly.

"I see what it is. You want to get rid of them, just because Mrs. Percy is pretty. You never want me to have anything to do with a pretty woman, as though I was still in swaddling bands. Dash it, Uncle, I reach my majority in six months."

"That leaves me only six months in which to ram some sense into you."

"But what is Mrs. Percy to do about coming and going? How can she get out of her cottage?" Bigelow demanded.

"I will be more than happy to arrange for her *going*—in my own carriage, if that is what it takes."

"You've got her locked up like a prisoner."

"She has two legs," Avedon pointed out. "In an emergency, she could walk or send a servant on shank's mare."

"She couldn't walk if she hurt herself," Bigelow said swiftly. "And supposing the place caught fire—dash it, it ain't safe. It's criminal irresponsibility."

"A fire?" Avedon said with interest. "Not a bad idea."

Bigelow, who was not much attuned to a joke, exclaimed, "You can't burn my cottage down!"

At this, Avedon burst into laughter. "No, cawker, I don't mean to go that far. Two or three days with no company and stale food will root them out."

"Well, it won't," Tony replied, and left on foot to cut across the brush and dust to Rose Cottage, to present his perspiring self to the ladies to commiserate with them.

"This is beyond anything," he apologized. "You will think we are a parcel of yahoos. Avedon is always interfering in my life, but to treat *you* in this manner—I hardly know what to say, Mrs. Percy."

"Call me Lucy," she said with a warm smile. "And help me, Tony." This was added in a wheedling tone that turned him rosy with pleasure. "Your uncle has marooned us—no milk or eggs this morning, so I cannot even offer you a cup of coffee or tea. We quite depended on Lady Sara's offer to supply us."

"I'll send some over from Milhaven, by Jove."

Lucy reached out and patted his hand. "So kind. I

knew we might depend on you. But Milhaven is three miles away, and inconvenient to be sending food every day."

"Yes, it's a pity you hadn't a couple of chickens and a cow," he agreed.

A light flashed in Lucy's eyes. "How clever you are! Of course, that is exactly what we need. Will you sell me some chickens and a cow?"

Tony beamed with pleasure. "No, *give* them. It is the least I can do."

This was even better, and Avedon would hear where she got them, too! "Do you know," Lucy said, "I think I must put in a little garden, there in front where you so thoughtfully thinned out the roses for us. You won't mind if we have to remove the grass as well?" A garden behind the house would not be offensive enough to anger Avedon, and all her stunts had the same goal of repaying him. "He cannot encroach on your property with his tiling."

Bigelow puffed up like a pigeon. "Just let him try it!"

"A garden wouldn't produce in time to do us any good," Mrs. Percy said with unusual crossness. The maddening persistence of the noise and dust were driving her to distraction. With all the windows closed, the house was like an oven, but still the dust was everywhere.

"I have a strange notion these tiles will set a new record for slowness in being laid," Lucy replied. "Where can I hire a couple of garden boys, Tony?"

"It won't be easy," he worried. "I see Avedon has

hired up every spare man in the neighborhood, along with his own men."

"The crew are your uncle's own men?" Lucy asked softly.

"Certainly. Who else should he use?"

"Who indeed?" Not a word was uttered about a crew from Canterbury.

"I'll send a couple of my own lads over, the Crawley brothers," Tony decided. "They're not bright fellows, but they'll do well enough to dig you up a garden."

The day was spent in a thoroughly enjoyable manner by Lucy, and incidentally by Avedon's crew, who had to admire the young lady's ingenuity. The cow was led on foot up the dusty, excavated road. The Crawley boys left off their digging to lay planks across the ditch and guide her to safety. Half a dozen hens were carried in, and the backhouse boy was sent off to the village on foot to order lumber and wire mesh for a henhouse, and seeds and seedlings for the garden. Lucy also had him post a letter to London, ordering her mount and phaeton. The latter she arranged to stable at Milhaven—and let us see how milord Avedon liked that! Certainly his nephew was tickled pink.

Tony stayed discreetly away from Chenely for a few days, and neither Avedon nor Lady Sara went near Rose Cottage. The latter was occupied with arranging her garden party, and Avedon stood too high on his dignity to be seen hanging around the meadow. The men continued moving earth around, making a deal of noise and generally having such a holiday as they had never before enjoyed. The Percys were much discussed at Chenely, but there was no direct news of them. The servants, who could have told them the whole tale, were reluctant to receive Avedon's wrath.

On the evening of the third day, Mrs. Percy's nerves were frayed from all the commotion, and she retired early to her dusty chamber. Avedon's frustration at not knowing what was going on reached a peak, and he had his mount saddled up. With great inconvenience he worked his way through the meadow to Rose Cottage. He arrived powdered in dust, with his hands pricked from a detour into nettles to reach the stable, and his cravat disarranged from branches flying against him. He surveyed with grim satisfaction the damage done to his road and the piles of earth all around the exterior of the cottage.

At the rear he saw one of Tony's milchers tethered to a post, grazing idly. He uttered a low curse just before his lips clenched angrily. The henhouse of wire and wood had been hastily constructed. Movement within told him it was already stocked. He went around to the front and stopped short. His eyebrows rose when he spotted the seedlings planted in what used to be a lawn. Mounds of dirt that surely held cucumbers had been formed along the west side. Other neat rows bespoke carrots and onions.

Very much accustomed to having his way, Avedon was vexed with the ladies' tactics. His nostrils pinched, but there was an unwilling wisp of admiration, too, at such high initiative and low cunning.

He fully expected to find Tony inside and went to the door ready to haul him out by the ear. He was greeted by a butler—such ostentation, a butler in a cottage—and shown into the parlor, where Lucy sat at the tambour frame in a state of the utmost serenity, to judge by her placid smile. The butler had alerted her to Avedon's arrival, and she had had time to compose herself.

"Good evening, Lord Avedon," she said very civilly, with just a glint of battle showing in her dark eyes. "So kind of you to drop by this evening." She cast a bland look at his disheveled toilette and said, "And what a job you had reaching us, too. You took pity at our being cut off, I assume?"

He batted at his dusty trousers while trying to think what to say. "Is Miss Percy out this evening?"

"How could she be? She doesn't have wings. She has retired early. The dust and noise bother her a little. If you feel your reputation can withstand sitting alone with me, I shall invite you to sit down."

"Thank you. I have no fear for *my* reputation."

"Nor I for mine," she said demurely. "My being a widow allows me a certain latitude in social matters." Avedon took a seat, and she continued, "Dear Tony usually accompanies me in the evening, but he has deserted me tonight."

This speech was intended to irritate her visitor, and did so to a satisfying degree. Avedon's brows rose and his lips tightened. "Indeed," he said.

"Oh, my, yes, I don't know what we should have done without him in our hour of distress. So very kind of him to insist on giving us a cow and hens, and supplying our every need now that we are cut off from the world. He sent over a couple of his men to put in our garden, just in case the laying of the tiles should be delayed. I daresay using your own untrained men instead of the crew from Canterbury must set the work back a little." Lucy continued plying her needle as she spoke.

Avedon was left without a word to say. His attack turned into a defense, and he muttered something about getting on with it, since the plans were made. "Where is Tony this evening?" he asked, to cover his embarrassment at being caught dead to rights.

"His mama returned late this afternoon," she replied. The incongruity of her telling him details of his own family delighted Lucy. "Cousin Morton came with her for a visit. You must forgive my calling him by such a familiar name, but Tony always calls him so, and I truly do not know whether Morton is his first or last name."

"Morton Carlton is his name."

"I should be learning these things." Lucy lifted her eyes from her work and smiled boldy at Avedon at this thrust, which conveyed that she hoped to join the family.

Avedon felt a burning sensation in his throat and said, "These details are not likely to be of much interest to you once you leave. Have you considered my offer to remove to another place? I have found a cottage quite similar to this—half timbered, with leaden windows."

"So very thoughtful of you, but we have no intention of removing at all. In fact, we like it so well we may spend our full twelve months here, and not just the summer as we originally planned."

He was through with controlling himself and flared into a towering rage. "You waste your time and money, madam, if you think to marry Lord Bigelow. When he enters into marriage, in ten years time, it will not be to a soldier's widow five or ten years his senior, but to a lady of his own kind and station."

"Tony tells me he is only six months short of reaching his majority. Your careful perusal of my face has misled you, sir. I am not thirty years old, nor even twenty-five, but scarcely twenty-two."

"I tell you quite frankly, your age is the least of your disadvantages. Your circumstances are in every way ineligible."

"You know nothing of my circumstances, sir."

"I know you are an officer's widow, living on your late husband's half pay. Don't try to con me, you are not wealthy. If there were property in the family, you would have some better place to go to than a hired cottage. Your social position is infinitely inferior to my nephew's, you are too old for him, and your manners are too free by half. Your persistence in hanging on where you are so patently not wanted will yield you nothing but a very disagreeable summer."

"I am wanted by your nephew," she pointed out. Lucy was so happy to have got Avedon into a pelter that she managed to control her own temper, though it was difficult.

"I am in control of my nephew," he said categorically. "I repeat my offer to move you elsewhere."

Lucy's nostrils dilated and she said in a tightly controlled tone, "Where was it you had in mind, milord? Coventry, perhaps?"

"We have already discussed a suitable destination at our former meeting. Tunbridge Wells is where I usually send Tony's flirts."

"Is it indeed? I take leave to tell you, Lord Avedon, that you will not send *me* there or anywhere else. I am here, and I shall stay. I have a signed contract for this hovel, for which I might add, I am paying an exorbitant five hundred pounds a year. Don't think I couldn't have Tony this month if I wanted him."

"I will be more than happy to refund the five hundred and another five hundred with it."

Lucy's eyes flashed dangerously and her color mounted. "Are you trying to buy me off! Yes, you are. I expect you have the check in your pocket, on which you have already stopped payment. I recognize that trick." She came to a gasping stop.

Avedon examined her with a sardonic grin. "I am surprised you choose to admit it, ma'am. No, I would not attempt to weasel out of payment on such an experienced shrew as yourself. How much did you screw out of your last victim?"

"Oh!" It was a squeal of outrage. "How dare you insult me under my own roof?"

"If you care to step outside, I will undertake to insult you more fully." Her hands were rigid, clasping and unclasping her skirt. Examining them, he noticed she wore no wedding ring and began to wonder if she was married at all.

"You could hardly do so!" Lucy charged angrily.

"Do you consider five hundred an insult? I'll make it a thousand, then. Mrs. Lacey, the local lightskirt, settled for five hundred last month. Tony would not have actually offered for her. She came hobbled with two children. Do you have any children, ma'am?"

"How should I have children when I'm not even—" Lucy clenched her jaws. "No, I have no children," she said grimly.

"Not even married, eh? Well, well. You find the guise of widow elicits sympathy from susceptible bantlings, I expect. There is much to be said for a maiden, however. There is just a little something about a secondhand woman. . . ."

Lucy rose majestically to her feet. "Get out," she said, pointing to the door. "I will not hear any more of your insults." Her breast rose and fell as she tried to contain her wrath.

Avedon remained seated, consciously adding an unspoken insult by doing so. Lucy stalked from the room and left him alone. Deserted, Avedon got up and sauntered toward the hallway. Lucy had said a word to the butler, and was just on her way upstairs.

She stopped and looked down over her shoulder, with fire flashing in her eyes. "Do pray tell your sister I look forward to seeing her at her garden party tomorrow, Lord Avedon. She invited Miss Percy and myself the day she arrived, and Tony is most eager for me to go and meet all his family."

Avedon was much impressed with her gall and sought quickly for a leveler. "Lady Sara managed to hire some extra girls from the village," he replied with a satirical smile. "She won't require your services to hand around the ices."

Lucy felt an overwhelming urge to stamp her foot, but quelled the childish impulse. "I am going, and don't think you can scare me away," she said, and continued on her way upstairs.

"I shall personally escort you off my property if you set one toe on it," he answered, but he didn't think she heard him. She neither turned around nor stopped but continued to her room.

Lucy longed to pour into her aunt's ears the iniquities that had been heaped on her head but did not like to disturb her. The man was a monster! To put her in the same class as Ronald Pewter—a fortune hunter. And to think she would have that silly twit of a Bigelow, whom she could hardly endure the sight of! To insult her under her own roof, to call her thirty years old, and to laugh so slyly when she let slip she wasn't married. To put her in a class with Mrs. Lacey, whoever *that* was! It was infamous.

She was of half a mind to marry Tony to show Avedon a lesson. And she would go to his sister's blasted garden party. What a temptation to put on an apron and go as a servant, still hanging on Tony's arm. It would serve him well. But she would not wear anything so unappealing. Her best garden bonnet, which framed her youthful face to a nicety, was what she would wear, and a flowing gown and a parasol. If the other local ladies were as unattractive as Lady Sara, she would put them all in the shade.

She had a strong desire to show Lord Avedon it was not only his nephew who found her attractive.

Lord Avedon had already made the discovery for himself. Mrs. Percy was younger than he thought. Twenty-two she claimed, and there was no point thinking she had lowered her age more than a year, if at all. She was also much too attractive for him to think he could control Tony if it came to a contest between them. A beauty was what the girl was. If he were not aware of her designs, he could fall in love with her himself. Not that he would ever marry such a creature. A strumpet, posing as a widow to curry pity from schoolboys. It was disgusting.

The war was a boon to her sort. They could claim alliance with some respectable person, dead and unable to defend himself. He'd look into this business of a Captain Percy. Ciudad Rodrigo Sal had mentioned as the place where the husband was supposed to have died. Perhaps if he confronted Tony with proof of her lies, he would see the light. He wondered if she would really attend Sal's garden party. He certainly did not put it a pace past her. To go setting up a farm on his doorstep to enable herself to remain, after all his work and expense to be rid of her. He had met a manager precariously close to being his own equal, but she wouldn't get her talons into Bigelow.

Chapter Seven

"Lady Sara has got beautiful weather for her garden party," Lucy said the next morning to her aunt. Lucy stuck by her intention to attend the party but felt her aunt would not go with her if she knew Lord Avedon's threat. It struck Lucy as better in every way that her aunt not attend, in case of unpleasantness.

"I forgot all about it!" Mrs. Percy exclaimed in consternation. "Tony has promised to send the Crawley boys to me this afternoon to weed out the back garden. I cannot leave them unattended after the shambles they made of the roses."

"We dare not leave them alone," Lucy agreed.

After a great deal of discussion, her aunt decided she must miss the party. "Be sure to make my excuses to Lady Sara," she said. "She will understand. It is so difficult to hire anyone, since Lord Avedon has employed every odd-job lad in the neighborhood.

I expect he added them to the Canterbury crew to hasten the work," she said, trying to make sense of it. "I daresay Tony will be happy to escort you, so you need not go alone."

Her niece said not a word to enlighten her. Tony used the loan of the Crawley brothers as an excuse to call in person at Rose Cottage that morning. He was delighted to escort Lucy, and after a hint or two from her, he suggested that his mama and Cousin Morton might as well go with them—a family party. No word was mentioned of Lord Avedon's visit the evening before.

Avedon was less circumspect in broadcasting his visit to Rose Cottage. He told Lady Sara the whole of it over breakfast. "The brazen hussy refuses to budge an inch. She has got a cow and a batch of hens from the idiot, and says she will see you at the garden party this afternoon."

"She would not be so bold!" Lady Sara gasped, delighted at such melodramatic doings. "I hope you let her know she will not be welcome."

"Ho, much she cares about welcome. She'll be here if she has to shoot her way in, and you may be sure she'll be hanging on the idiot's arm, so we can hardly ask her to leave."

"No, Tony will come with Isabel and Cousin Morton."

"Possibly. But what shall we do if she comes?" Avedon asked.

Lady Sara gave it her deep consideration. "We can hardly turn them off after I invited them. We shall give them a cold shoulder, and the neighborhood will see what we think of women of Mrs. Percy's kidney."

"You aren't fully aware of the nature of her kidney, either. I don't believe she was ever married at all," Avedon said. "She let something slip last night."

Lady Sara promptly demanded all the details. "She may not even be a Percy for all we know," she said after the tale was unfolded.

"She could be anyone. There is a respectable family of Percys at Dorset, but I doubt she's any kin to them. You know that fellow in Hampshire who was in the Peninsula, Sal. Can you find out form him if there was a Captain Percy there, and if he was married?"

"Yes, George Wesley lost an arm, poor soul. I shall write to his mama this very day. Mrs. Percy is a scheming woman, come here to snap up Tony, but we shall soon be rid of her. How could she have heard of him, Adrian? Your advertisement was so discreetly worded."

"Mrs. Lacey, perhaps. No doubt the muslin company has a freemasonry amongst themselves to share word of their victims. If they have, Tony's name must be at the top of their list. It is a great pity Mrs. Percy is so attractive. She just might succeed in nabbing him."

Lady Sara shot a suspicious glance at her brother, but Adrian was not susceptible to upstarts. He held too high an opinion of himself for that. If Adrian had a fault, which was by no means positive, it was pride. His angry face assured her he was in no danger from Mrs. Percy, no matter how pretty she was.

77

"We shan't worry any more about it till we see whether she comes. Her sister-in-law may deter her. She, at least, seems well-bred. Of more importance to me is my husband. He deserves that appointment, Adrian. And after he is archdeacon, he will be a bishop. It is only right that he should be called a lord, for *I* am *Lady* Sara. He'll never manage it by himself. All he thinks of is the church; it is for us to make the connections. I am sure that a word dropped in the right ear would secure the appointment for him. Papa's old friend, Judge Almont, is acquainted with the archbishop, is he not?" The conversation turned to the other inevitable subject, and Mrs. Percy was forgotten.

With a letter to write to Hampshire and the arrangement of a garden party that must eclipse every other garden party in the county, the morning was a busy one for Lady Sara. There were the ices, always a dreadful nuisance but essential, as no one else served them. There was the punch, and the squeezing of three dozen lemons for lemonade, and only two squeezers in the whole house. There were the meat pies and lobster patties for the adults and sandwiches for the children. Cakes and petits fours and cream buns had to be tasted for freshness and quality—no tiresome part of the morning for Lady Sara, who enjoyed tooth work.

On top of her other duties she had to examine the grounds for signs of slovenly gardening, to count the chairs and tables and see all was in order. One hundred and four bentwood chairs. One hundred was such a nice round number that she decided to take the four extra back to Hampshire with her. And perhaps that little iron-topped table for the rose garden. She found little fault with anything. Say that for Adrian, his house and grounds were properly maintained. As to the kitchen, though, it was a shame for the waste that went on. Four hams in the larder. One would never be missed when she left.

At two o'clock the crowd began to arrive. At two-thirty, with his eyes weary from scanning the gate for Mrs. Percy, Avedon began to relax and think she had decided to stay away. His first swell of satisfaction gave way to regret as two-thirty turned into two forty-five. It was a demmed dull party after all. Mrs. Percy had scored a minor victory. She had kept Tony and his family away. Avedon wondered what they were all doing. Lady Beatrice got hold of his arm for a "nice little coze," as she invariably described her endless gossip.

It was a quarter of an hour later that he saw Tony romping toward him. His mother and Cousin Morton were with him, but Avedon paid them little heed. It was at Mrs. Percy, hanging on Tony's arm, that he and most of his guests stared. She wore a charming bonnet with pink rosebuds around the brim, and a fine white gown with a broad pink sash. Long pink kid gloves picked up the color of the trim and looked stunning. She might have stepped out of a Fragonard painting into his garden.

Avedon could almost forgive the besotted smile Tony wore. How vibrant and alive she looked, how young and lovely. Say that for the muslin company, they knew how to make themselves look attractive.

Lady Beatrice tugged at his elbow, and he turned perforce to her. The contrast was strikingly obvious. She was past the first blush of youth and hopelessly plain. In fact, as he reviewed his female acquaintances, Avedon realized there wasn't a real dasher in the parish. No wonder Tony trailed after the other sort.

"Is this Tony's latest flirt?" Lady Beatrice asked in a sarcastic voice.

Avedon felt a strong and inexplicable urge to defend the interloper. "It is his new tenant, Mrs. Percy," he said stiffly.

Before long the desire to defend was swept away. Mrs. Percy was clearly in no need of defense. She came sashaying forward with a bold, glinting smile. "Lord Avedon, I am come, as I promised you last night when you called," she said.

Lady Beatrice pokered up. Avedon calling on this commoner?

Avedon performed a brisk bow. "Good afternoon, ma'am. Has your sister-in-law not come?"

"She is taking advantage of Tony's kind offer to loan her a couple of gardeners. Workmen are unaccountably hard to find this season," she replied. Her flashing eyes reminded him of the reason. "Lady Bigelow and Mr. Carlton and Tony took pity on me and asked me to come with them," she added. The smiles of her companions told Avedon they knew nothing of what was going on. Morton Carlton, in particular, looked fascinated, and he was a gentleman who had vast experience of ladies.

As he approached his fortieth year, an attractive frosting of silver decorated the hair around his temples. His face showed some incipient signs of aging, but he wore his wrinkles so debonairly that they appeared an added attraction. His dark, dangerous eyes, his vulpine smile, and his excellent tailoring set him quite apart from the provincial gentlemen.

"It is a pity about Mrs. Percy's road being dug up," Mr. Carlton said. "I was just telling her she ought to come to Milhaven till it is mended. It shouldn't be more than a day or two."

"You tempt me, Mr. Carlton," Lucy said, with a batting of her long lashes in his direction.

"We would be very happy to have you, I'm sure," Lady Bigelow said, smiling. The dame was a byword for foolishness. Avedon thought it exactly like Isabel to invite a scheming hussy into her home to seduce her son.

"That would be inconvenient to Mrs. Percy, since she has set up a farm," Avedon replied.

"The servants could take care of the cow and my few hens," Lucy assured him. "I am considering Lady Bigelow's kind offer. If the road is not usable *very soon*, I shall remove to Milhaven."

Avedon read the note of warning in her seemingly innocent remark. She had him over a barrel, and they both knew it. "I shall make it top priority," he told her, swallowing the gall of defeat and forcing himself to put a smiling face on it. He looked as if he were eating a lemon.

"I was sure you would. So kind of you, Lord Avedon."

"I am happy to hear it," Mr. Carlton said, "as I for one plan to make many calls at Rose Cottage, and I'm sure Isabel will accompany me."

Lady Bigelow smiled vaguely and said to Lady Beatrice, "No flies this year. The place is usually swarming with them for Sally's garden party. This year she has provided dust instead. It must have blown in from the meadow."

"You do not have anything to drink, Mrs. Percy," Lady Beatrice mentioned during a lull in conversation.

"Are you short of servant girls, Lord Avedon?" Lucy said to him. "I was sure you told me last night you had sufficient. Had I known you were short, I would have put on my apron and offered to give you a hand," she said playfully.

"Would you care for an ice, Mrs. Percy?" he asked, with lips tensed at her impertinence.

"Indeed I would, for the dust *does* catch in one's throat. But that will soon be taken care of." Under Lady Beatrice's outraged nose, the widow waltzed off with Lord Avedon, to be served an ice.

"You have won the battle, not the war," he warned her.

"I am assembling my forces, sir. If I find Milhaven a more strategic position from which to wage battle, you may be sure I shan't hesitate to relocate. Or should I say advance my forces?"

"Why didn't you go? It must have served your purpose admirably." He was puzzled at her refusal.

"You don't know what my fell purpose is. As I am a captain's widow, you must be on the alert for deep maneuvering on my part."

"Surely you are here to trap Bigelow into an offer of marriage?" He was handed an ice and gave it to Lucy.

She accepted and tasted it before answering. "Trap him? You make him sound like an animal. How conceited you men are. You think marriage is all we have on our minds. This is a very good ice, by the way."

She looked strangely youthful and innocent, like a little girl, licking her ice. "If not that, why *are* you here?" Avedon inquired.

"I am recovering my health, as I explained in my letter."

"You look perfectly healthy to me."

"Thank you. And now shall we remove the gloves, milord? We are far enough removed that the others cannot hear us. I am here on your turf, against your explicit orders. Do you mean to usher me to the gate, as threatened, or has your nerve failed you? It is poor policy to utter ultimatums unless one intends to keep them. Otherwise you will never be taken seriously."

"So, you *did* hear me. I wasn't sure."

"It was my lungs that were ailing, not my ears. You didn't answer my question."

"I hope I am not such a barbarian as that."

"No, indeed. You are so gentlemanly, you only call me a lightskirt when we are alone," she reminded him. "I would think less badly of you if you did as you threatened."

"As we are alone, Mrs. Percy—or whatever your name is—I don't hesitate to say I rescind nothing that I said last night."

"Except, perhaps, your threat of showing me the gate? That is two battles for me, *n'est-ce pas?* Oh, Tony, are you looking for me?"

Bigelow, fast pelting toward them, wore the angry expression of a child whose toy has been snatched from him. He was clearly looking for Mrs. Percy and was not happy to find her alone with his uncle. He lowered his brows at Avedon and took Lucy's arm jealously to introduce her to Kent's society as "my dear friend, Mrs. Percy."

Lady Sara came running to her brother to discover what had transpired. "What is to be done?" she demanded in a fierce whisper. "Isabel tells me she has invited Mrs. Percy to Milhaven. This must not be allowed, Avedon." Lady Sara called her brother Avedon when she wished to be dramatic.

"I'd like to keep this story as close to home as possible. Mrs. Percy has no intention of accepting the invitation."

"Of course she will, simpleton! There is nothing the trollop would like better than to get a toe into Milhaven. She will become a tenant for life if she does."

"No, she says if I repair the road, she won't go."

"But why not? It is some trick, depend on it."

"We have a few tricks up our sleeve, too, Sal. Did you send that letter to your friend in Hampshire?"

"I sent it off in today's mail. In a few days, we'll know."

"Then we have only to lull her suspicions for a few days. Once we have proof she's lying, we can force her out." A smile of satisfaction settled on Avedon's swarthy face. His embattled pride looked forward to finally winning the war with Mrs. Percy.

Lady Sara peered around her brother's shoulder to spy on the widow. "Just look how Tony is making up to her, in the most obvious and ill-bred way, holding her ice for her to eat. There, now Cousin Morton is joining them. You must have noticed that he has an eye for her as well. Morton always had a colt's tooth in his head."

Avedon examined the spectacle for himself. "Morton has both eyes on her, and so has every other gentleman here. Surely with such a surfeit of admirers, we can find someone to replace Tony in her scheme."

"You are the only other title. That, I fancy, is Tony's special attraction."

"I wonder." He frowned at Mr. Carlton. "If it's only a good match she has in mind, she might think to nab Morton. He's rich as Croesus, and not quite over the hill yet. Fortyish, isn't he?"

"Thirty-nine, but he won't tumble for her."

"Are you blind?" Avedon demanded. "Why is it a lady never knows who men find attractive? He's like a fly after honey—but he won't *marry* her."

"That's what I meant, obviously," Lady Sara replied with a sneer.

A satirical grin took possession of Avedon's features. "I'll slip Morton word what she's up to. He'll enjoy having an excuse to dangle after her, and it will put him on his guard in the unlikely case he develops any serious ideas. It is the perfect way to save Tony. I think this is one battle for us, Sal."

"I wonder if Cousin Morton knows the archbishop," Lady Sara said. "Or the master of Lazarus College—he traffics in ecclesiastical appointments. A word in his ear—"

"They're all Tories at Oxford, as blue as your blood," her brother said.

"I cannot think you are really exerting yourself on John's behalf, Avedon," Lady Sara snipped, and went off to pull Cousin Morton away from Mrs. Percy, who was interfering inordinately in John's appointment.

Chapter Eight

"You're mad," Mr. Carlton said bluntly, when Avedon got him alone at the party and outlined the nature of his suspicions against Mrs. Percy. "I hope I know a lady when I see one. She is country from head to heels, but she is genteel country. And she isn't after Tony in the least. She spends half her time swatting him down."

"And the other half urging him on," Avedon pointed out. "He doesn't leave her skirt tails for a minute, Morton. He's the laughingstock of the place. First Lacey, now this one."

"I expect it's the Lacey affair that has got you in the boughs, but you're high into the realms of imagination to compare the two women. In the first place Mrs. Percy wouldn't have such a high stickler for a chaperon if she were not a genuine lady. And in the second she'd have picked up on Tony's offer to move into Milhaven so fast your head would spin. No, no, you're far off the mark, Avedon," Carlton said firmly.

"You haven't been privileged to hear how she carries on when Tony's not around. She as well as told me she meant to have him."

Carlton just smiled and shook his head. "No doubt you got her dander up with your stiff-rumped ways." Avedon looked offended. "Only your best friends dare to tell you. You can't help it, Avedon. Your papa was the same, but—"

"Papa! I am not like *him*!"

"Cut from the same bolt. It has taken some lady of spirit like Mrs. Percy to tackle you. She is not shy, I'll grant you that."

"The woman is insolent."

"No, Avedon, the *lady* is outspoken. I have no use for simpering misses myself. And another thing, she would not have come to a little backwater like this if she were after a gent. She'd have gone to some bustling watering spot."

"She discovered in some way that Tony was here, ripe for plucking," Avedon explained.

Mr. Carlton batted the idea away in disgust. "Use your head, man. How could she know? Bigelow is not that rich or famous. Did you use his title in the advertisement?"

"I'm not that big a fool. I used a box number."

"There you are, then. She had no notion he was here, or you, either.

"I didn't say she was throwing her bonnet at me."

"But why wouldn't she, Avedon? Your fortune and title are both greater than Tony's, yet she hasn't made any effort to seduce you. Is that what has piqued your pride?" he asked laughingly.

"Don't be an ass."

Mr. Carlton bowed playfully. "I'll try not to follow your example, Cousin. As it happens, you are only urging me to do what I had already decided to do—namely, cut Tony out."

"While making sure Mrs. Percy does not cut you in," Avedon added with a warning look.

"A fate worse than death, what? To be caught by such an antidote. I'll tell you this, Avedon. If she were a filly, I'd buy her." He looked around the grounds till he spotted Mrs. Percy and went off after her. Lucy greeted him with obvious pleasure.

Avedon stood on a moment alone, watching them from the distance and thinking. Why *hadn't* Mrs. Percy exerted any effort to please him? He was an earl, the owner of three sprawling and extremely profitable estates, yet the woman had not once flirted with him. Was he so repulsive that not even his extreme eligibility could tempt her? Between Sally and Tony, she must certainly have received an idea of his position, yet she went out of her way to irritate him.

His plan of setting Morton onto the widow had succeeded beyond his best expectations, yet Avedon was dissatisfied. He was sorry Morton was quite so dashing and handsome. Mrs. Percy would switch beaux with no reluctance, he fancied, yet he took very little pleasure from the knowledge.

He took even less pleasure the next morning in the village to see Mrs. Percy seated in Mr. Carlton's stylish tilbury. She nodded to him with a pert smile, and Morton pulled the team to a halt to talk. Morton, the dog, looked ten years younger. What the devil had he done to himself? That rose in his lapel— surely it came from Rose Cottage? It matched the blossoms in his waistcoat. When Morton lifted his curled beaver, Avedon noticed his hair was arranged more stylishly. He had it brushed forward in the Brutus do to conceal the silvering in front. But it was the rakish grin on his lips that lent him that devil-may-care air of attraction. Sally was always saying Cousin Morton was handsome, but till that morning he hadn't thought so himself.

"Good morning, folks. A lovely day," Avedon said, lifting his hat and trying for a light air to match the mood of the others.

"I am surprised you aren't on the estate, wielding the whip over your workers, Avedon," Morton joked.

"It happens I had business with my solicitor," Avedon replied.

"We did not for a moment imagine it was pleasure that drew you into town," Lucy said pertly.

Between the pair of them, they were making him sound like a philistine. "Business before pleasure," he said, feeling foolish.

"What mad frolic do you have planned for the afternoon?" Morton inquired with an air of railery. "A meeting with the vicar to discuss parish doings? Or is it the day for you to interview the keeper of the local orphanage?"

Neither of these meetings was planned, but Avedon regretted that he hadn't something dashing to offer. "Actually I am calling on Lady Beatrice," he lied, for he wanted to bring a lady's name into the conversation to show that he was at least acquainted with dalliance.

Morton just shook his head. "There is no accounting for taste," he said. "I'll leave you to her. Let us flee, Mrs. Percy, before he shanghais us into accompanying him. We can find something more amusing to do this fine day. Give her my regards, Avedon."

He whipped up the team and sped away. As Avedon got into his carriage, he felt completely dissatisfied not only with the brief meeting but with his whole life. It was a fine thing when a man couldn't come up with one attractive female acquaintance. It was his having missed the London season that accounted for it. And that, like everything else, was Tony's fault.

On his way back to Chenely he stopped at Rose Cottage to see how the work was progressing. The road was half-restored; the men weren't breaking their backs to get it finished. Being at the house, he decided to stop in and talk to Miss Percy and see if he could discover anything of interest from her.

She made him welcome politely. With her gray hair covered in a lace cap and her body in a dark gown, she was the very picture of respectability. Avedon had several such relatives himself, and in spite of his suspicions, he was soon on a good footing with her. Obviously the widow had not revealed his rudeness, or her chaperon would not be treating him so civilly. He felt a stab of guilt at his hypocrisy.

"So kind of you to stop by," Mrs. Percy said.

"We were sorry you could not attend the garden party yesterday, ma'am," he replied.

"I was most eager to set my own garden to rights," she explained, and chatted about her hobby for some minutes. "But I am happy Lucy could attend. She needs some socializing, after two deaths in the family coming so closely together."

"Who has she lost, besides her husband?" he asked with quickening interest. He had been hoping to turn the conversation to Mrs. Percy.

"Her father died not half a year after Captain Percy's death. Her husband's father, that is to say," she added in confusion. "She was staying with Alex's family in Dorset while he was in the Peninsula."

"It is the Dorset Percys she is connected with, then!" he exclaimed.

"Yes, we are the Dorset Percys," the dame said, with a touch of pride. It was an old and good family, though not noble. She took her husband's family for her own, to keep the story straight. She and Lucy had decided that the details of their life should remain as they were, except for the few necessary adjustments regarding fortune and marital status.

"And you have lost a father and a brother. I am very sorry, ma'am. Why did not you and Mrs. Percy return to—"

"Fernbank," she said, supplying the name for him.

"I hope you don't object to my asking?"

"Not at all. My father sold the estate when Alexander died. We two ladies were ill prepared to run a large estate, you must know. He felt cash would be less troublesome for us." This came perilously close to admitting that Lucy was an heiress, and she spoke on to dilute the notion. "It was expensive to keep up, of course, and mortgaged, too."

Avedon was more confused than ever. The lady's story had the ring of truth, and if so, they had all been doing Mrs. Percy an injustice. The only possible explanation left was that the captain had married miserably beneath him. He said, "Mrs. Percy was also from Dorset, I expect? An old friend of the family?"

Her aunt quickly moved her next door and changed her into Alex's sweetheart. "Yes, she was a Walcott before marriage. Another old Dorset family. We have known them for years."

He was stymied. Had he painted a perfectly respectable lady into a scheming monster on no grounds but prejudice? Made her into another Lacey, from overrated fears for Tony's safety?

Miss Percy served him a glass of lemonade and gingerbread, which somehow confirmed in him the idea that they were both perfectly respectable, honest country people. He apologized for the inconvenience of the road being dug up and pointed out that it would soon be repaired.

"And after all your work, you did not get your tiles laid," she commented with more sorrow than anger. "The Canterbury crew had to leave, I take it?"

Avedon blushed for his mendacity. "A large contractor reneged on a deal, but at the last minute it was salvaged, so my work is put off till next year." And who is the lying scoundrel in this case? he asked himself silently.

Miss Percy accepted it without a word of censure, and before long Avedon was on his way, reviewing what he had heard. He was much inclined to think he had been overly zealous in protecting Tony. Morton, who knew about such things, said the widow had no interest in him. Her refusing an invitation to Milhaven substantiated it. He had behaved abominably to her and was eager to set the matter to rights. He particularly regretted having set Morton on her. At least his cousin realized she was a lady and not someone with whom he could take liberties.

When he reached Chenely, Tony was there waiting for him with a face a mile long. "Morton is cutting you out, is he?" Avedon asked. His tone was more kindly than usual.

"She doesn't like *him*!" Tony answered, fire in his eye. "She would have driven out with me if Morton hadn't got up at the crack of dawn and beat me to Rose Cottage. Her chaperon told me she only went with him because he knew someone who knew her husband, and she wanted to talk about that."

"Morton knows something about her husband! I am happy we have discovered someone who does."

"Well he don't, if you want the truth. It is all a hum to catch her interest."

Another liar in the family, Avedon noted, and felt a degree worse. "Where were they going?"

"He's taking Lucy over to Plimpton's farm to get her a puppy."

"Why does she want a dog? Have the men digging up the road been giving her trouble?" he asked, ready to assume more guilt.

"No, it's only a pet. A little spaniel pup."

"We have a whole litter here. She could have had one of ours if we knew she wanted a dog." Avedon felt offended that she had not asked.

"She'd not be apt to ask *you* for anything." Tony sulked. "You snapping at her and lashing your tail every time you hear her name."

Adrian just frowned and walked away. Tony was an idiot, but even idiots occasionally speak the truth. Later Avedon discussed his visit to Rose Cottage with his sister, and told her he believed he had done the girl an injustice.

Sally gave a disparaging look. "Why, only because they *say* they are the Dorset Percys? It is a good, safe distance away. We are not likely to be able to check up easily. If Mr. Percy sold his estate, why did Mrs. Percy not go to her own home? You said she was a neighbor, did you not?"

"I hadn't thought of that," Avedon admitted. It was a good point, and enough to cast some doubt on the tale Miss Percy had told him. Avedon was in a vacillating frame of mind, sorry at times he had treated the widow so ill, and angry to the point of fury at others at her goings on.

He called twice at the cottage over the next few days, but did not manage to catch Mrs. Percy at home. She was always out with either Tony or Morton. His visits to the village increased, and he twice saw her, once in Tony's curricle, and the second time in Morton's tilbury. When she cast a triumphant smile at him, he felt a pronounced desire to pull her down and shake her.

Mrs. Percy was less discussed at Chenely than formerly. Lady Sara was easy in her mind that Tony had been saved for Prissy, for of the widow's two suitors, Morton now clearly had the upper hand. Morton was by no means to be traded off for Tony; his fortune, too, must be kept in the family, preferably by his remaining single and leaving his money to some of her numerous progeny. As well as Prissy Lady Sara had three strapping boys to be provided for. But Morton was a man of the world. A gentleman of mature years who had evaded the snares of such persistent wooers as Lady Beatrice was felt to be in no danger of succumbing to a captain's widow.

Avedon was less certain of Morton's safety. His visit to Milhaven had been for the purpose of delivering Lady Bigelow home. He would normally have left within a day or two. He gave no sign of leaving and made no pretense that his reason for clinging on was anything but Mrs. Percy. He had developed an oddly uncharacteristic way of acting and dressing—consciously youthful. On the few occasions when Adrian or Sally saw him, they teased him about his new Brutus do and brighter waistcoats, but he was unfazed.

"I ain't over the hill yet, Sal," he said, laughing. "Don't count on my bankroll. I am thinking of setting up my own nursery."

"Oh, Morton, at your age," she scoffed.

"I am only in my thirties, like young Adrian here."

"A slip of a boy of thirty-nine, with a birthday in October," she reminded him.

"A groom of forty would look foolish," he said. A

smile lifted his lips at Sally's nodding agreement. "I must get cracking and do the thing up before October." This was said in a joking spirit, yet the assiduity with which he was courting Mrs. Percy raised doubts in Avedon's bosom.

These doubts reached a new height when Morton casually mentioned attending an assembly in Ashford. He hadn't bothered with the local assemblies for a decade.

"You can't mean you are going to that!" Adrian exclaimed in amazement.

"Mrs. Percy wishes to attend, and I have offered to escort her."

"Oh, Morton, my dear," Sally chided. "You will look an utter quiz, dancing at your age. The whole village is already tittering at this strange way you drag your hair forward. I cannot think it necessary. You are not that bald."

"I am not bald at all, just graying a little."

Lady Sara gave another of her rueful smiles at such self-delusion. "The whole town will be in whoops, to see a man your age up jigging with a young girl."

Morton flicked a mote of dust from his sleeve. "I'm not quite ready for the urn yet. Was it not Mrs. Percy's advanced years that were used as one of the many excuses for her ineligibility when it was Tony who had the inside track?" he asked.

"There was no need for excuses!" Sally fired back. "There are good and sufficient reasons for finding her entirely ineligible."

"I don't find an attractive young widow from a

good family so ineligible as you do. But you may stop worrying about Tony. She won't marry him."

"She won't marry you, either," Avedon said angrily.

"*Tut, tut,* Cousin. I ain't a cawker under your heavy thumb. It was you who set me onto her, so don't cry craven on me now." He drew out his watch and glanced at it. "This has been delightful, but I have an engagement with Mrs. Percy, and I would not like to keep her waiting." He rose and sauntered from the room, leaving his angry cousins behind.

Chapter Nine

Lady Sara was thrown into alarm by these ominous signs of Morton's fortune escaping the fold. "I think we must attend this wretched assembly ourselves, Adrian," she said.

"I plan to attend."

She looked startled. "Why, you never go unless you have company visiting, and even then you complain like the devil."

"I'll be at this one," he said grimly.

"Good, and if Morton is making too much headway with the widow, you must cut him out."

Avedon adjusted his cravat and said with arrogant nonchalance, "That had occurred to me as one solution."

"For, of course, *you* would never be vulnerable to such a creature," Sally said with a steely, commanding look.

On this occasion it was Avedon who was eager to

turn to the other topic of conversation. "Was Morton any help in nudging John's promotion along?"

"The obstinate creature says he doesn't know the archbishop. I'm sure he does, but he will never stir a finger to help anyone."

Mrs. Percy received a letter from Bishop Norris announcing that he would be stopping at Canterbury on his way home from the conference at Lambeth Palace and suggesting that she and Lucy meet him there. Unaware of how well the ladies were entertained, he thought he was giving them a treat. He promised to give them a tour of the famous cathedral, a project that had often been discussed in the past. He would also stay with them a few days at Rose Cottage before continuing to St. Giles.

"What shall we do about Lady Sara?" Mrs. Percy asked Lucy. "She will recognize him in an instant. Her husband is at St. Giles. She has no fondness for the bishop."

"She hasn't called on us in an age," Lucy pointed out.

"But if she does—I cannot like to ask a bishop to lie."

"No lies are necessary," Lucy said. "There is no reason we cannot be related to a bishop. He knows I am posing as Mrs. Percy and won't say anything to give us away. You bother yourself for nothing, Auntie. It will be lovely to see Uncle Norris again."

"Well, I daresay he will be fagged to death and only means to rusticate a day or two in the quiet of the country. Shall I tell him we'll meet him at Canterbury?"

"Yes, why not? It will be a little change—or do you dread the trip?"

Mrs. Percy hid her dread as much as she could and said she would write a note arranging the rendezvous at Canterbury. The visit was temporarily forgotten in the excitement of the Ashford assembly.

The inhabitants of Ashford were agreeably surprised to see both the noble families of the neighborhood turn out in force for their little assembly. The entire ménage of both Milhaven and Chenely were there. Of equal interest were the newcomers from Rose Cottage. They attended with the Milhaven party, and Lucy caused a great sensation when she arrived in such elevated company, wearing a seagreen froth of chiffon, with diamonds sparkling at her throat and ears.

"Diamonds," Lady Sara said in a dismissing voice to her brother. They had arrived five minutes before the Milhaven party and were watching the door eagerly. "I wonder who she got them from. They look dreadfully out of place at a simple country assembly. I shall slip her the hint she is overdressed. A common mistake amongst parvenues."

"Lady Beatrice is wearing hers," Avedon mentioned.

"Ah, is dear Beatrice here? How did I miss her?"

"You cannot have been looking very hard. She takes up the pair of chairs right across from us."

She slapped her brother's wrist playfully. "Don't make fun of your own partner, Adrian. You and Beatrice will be leading off. She looks charming. I'm

101

amazed she can still squeeze into that old peacock-blue gown. I swear it came off the ark."

He glanced glumly across the hall to where Lady Beatrice was just rising. She was an unappetizing vision in blue, with her jet-black hair piled into a mountain on top of her head. She looked about as lively as an oyster on the half shell. His eyes moved again to Mrs. Percy. He had seen her in motion, and knew her trim and fashionable figure would move gracefully on the dance floor. With a heavy heart Avedon strode across the room to Lady Beatrice.

It was uncharitably said of Lady Beatrice that she would marry if she had to have the village idiot. This was not entirely accurate, but her escorts were drawn from a wide spectrum of society. She was delighted to have a gentleman worthy of her for once at a local assembly. "Avedon, we are greatly honored this evening," she smiled. Her teeth seemed to get longer by the year. "I see the Milhaven party is enlarged by two. I am shocked at Isabel dragging that girl along with her."

"I expect it was the gentlemen who did the dragging," he replied dampingly.

"More likely the widow. The *on dit* is that she has switched her attack from Tony to Morton. Well, she was aiming a little high to try for a title."

"Do you think so, Beatrice? I think she might aim as high as she likes," he answered blightingly and took her pudgy arm to lead her to the floor.

Morton was not far behind them, accompanied by Mrs. Percy. Tony turned to a group of chattering young ladies just returned from the seminary and spotted a Miss Evans with limpid blue eyes and blond curls. The girl had improved vastly over the past ten months, and he honored her with his arm. As soon as the set was over, he was after Lucy.

She was happy to stand up with him, but when he continued pestering her at the set's end, she looked about for help. The only three gentlemen with whom she was acquainted were Morton, Tony, and Avedon. The locals hung back, as she had acquired a vicarious air of nobility due to her company. Across the hall Avedon noticed her problem and used it as an excuse to approach her.

"Is the whelp bothering you?" he asked ungraciously, when he saw Tony's downcast expression. Tony turned and stalked off in a huff.

Lucy felt an excited churning in her breast and readied herself for verbal battle. "How can you say so, milord? You must know it is always I who bother Bigelow," she replied pertly.

Avedon was unaware that he was smiling. It softened the harshness of his features and even lent him an air of flirtation. "Now you are bothering Morton, so we have forgiven you," he said, and took her hand. He had forgotten to ask her if she would stand up with him.

"You have decided Morton is expendable, have you?" she asked.

"Not entirely, but at his age he is capable of defending himself." He put a proprietary hand on her elbow and began walking onto the floor.

Lucy decided Avedon was being just a trifle high in the instep and decided to roast him. "Where are we going?" she asked.

"I thought you would like to dance," he said. No fear of possible refusal disturbed his thoughts. He was Lord Avedon. In the entire course of his life, no lady had ever refused his attentions.

"You have misread my likes before, Lord Avedon." He stopped and looked a question at her. "If you had bothered to ask me, I could have saved you the embarrassment of leaving you stranded alone in the middle of the floor," she said, and removed her hand from his arm.

"But why did you come if you don't want to dance?"

"I *do* want to dance, but a lady has the prerogative of declining any partner who does not please her," she said demurely.

He saw the mischief glinting in her smile. "Would it please you if I humbly requested the pleasure of standing up with you, Mrs. Percy?"

"The 'humbly' pleases me," she bantered. "Even if you don't mean it. Since I know so few gentlemen here this evening, it is either dancing with you or warming a chair by the wall."

He bowed with mock seriousness. "I am flattered that you prefer my company to that of a block of wood. Has your road been repaired satisfactorily? I told my steward to see to it."

"Yes, and it is a great pity that no tiles were laid, after such a deal of trouble."

"It was no trouble."

"It was for me," she objected. "Had you ever any intention of laying tiles at all?"

"I mean to do it one day."

His offhand answer was as good as an admission that he had only dug up the road to annoy her. "It was an underhanded trick, sir. I wonder that you thought to get rid of us by such a paltry device."

"It was only the first step. I was going to pour salt in your well next, but my steward was afraid it would bleed back into my own water," he admitted with no sign of shame.

"Well, upon my word!"

When he stopped and looked down at her, Lucy saw the laughter lurking in his eyes and didn't know whether she was angry or amused. "I have apologized to Miss Percy for my error, and now I apologize to you. I am very sorry I inconvenienced you with my underhanded, paltry trick."

Lucy tossed her curls. "So you should be."

"It goes sadly against the pluck for me to apologize, Mrs. Percy. The least you could do is accept it with generosity."

With the taste of victory sweet in her mouth, Lucy accepted it. "You are forgiven, then," she said.

"Thank you. Now let us begin our acquaintance anew and see if we cannot rub along like two civilized adults this time. You look very charming this evening, ma'am."

"Thank you, milord. You look quite decent yourself, when I see your face without a scowl for the first time in my life."

His smile stretched to a grin, for Avedon was delighted to finally achieve a friendly footing with the most charming lady in the room. "Have I really been that ferocious?" he asked, inclining his head toward her.

"You remind me of the wild animals at the Exchange."

Avedon cocked his head aside and frowned. "Surely not all of them! Which one did you have in mind?"

"The bear," she replied instantly.

He patted her fingers in a familiar way. "Try honey," he suggested. "That always turns a bear up sweet."

Lucy felt a flush suffuse her cheeks at his manner. "I am not trying to make a tame pet of you, sir! A little civility is all I want."

"Your menagerie at Rose Cottage becomes crowded, does it?" he joked. "If the animals become tiresome, you must come to Chenely and escape them for an afternoon."

"I have been severely hinted away from that prestigious pile of stones by the owner," she reminded him. "And his character is such that I dare not disobey."

"You flouted his orders to stay away from the garden party. If he ordered you to keep out of his house, would you disobey that, too?"

"If he sees fit to issue such an order, we shall see."

"You have piqued my curiosity, Mrs. Percy. I hereby order you not to come for dinner tomorrow evening, and not to bring your sister-in-law with you."

Lucy was thoroughly amazed to find such an accomplished flirt hiding beneath Avedon's harsh exterior. She feared he might revert to his old nature at any moment and hardly knew how far she might push him. "We shall have to wait for another occasion to test my docility. I am having dinner at Milhaven tomorrow."

Avedon's voice held an edge when he next spoke. "At Tony's or Morton's request?"

"Why, it is usually the hostess who issues invitations. Lady Bigelow asked us."

Frustrated in his attempt to learn which gentleman held the lead, he pressed on with his own overtures. "The next day, then. Are you free not to come to Chenely then?"

Lucy remembered her Uncle Norris's visit and preparations for the trip to Canterbury. "No, I am quite busy this week."

"Oh, doing what and with whom?" he asked, quite as though it were any of his business.

"Entertaining a gentleman," Lucy said unhelpfully. "We designing widows, you know, do not waste our time on ladies."

"Is another apology called for?" he asked, with a disarming smile.

"If you truly think I came here to angle after your nephew, it is. You have completely misjudged my motives in running to ground. I came to escape a gentleman, not to chase one."

"How intriguing! And the visiting gentleman—he is not the one you wish to evade, I assume?"

"Certainly not!"

Curiosity robbed Avedon of his manners, and he quizzed her bluntly. "Is it because of this unwanted gentleman that you don't return to Dorset?"

"No, Fernbank was sold, as I believe Miss Percy has already told you."

"I meant return to your own home. Surely your family—the Walcotts, isn't it?—would be happy to welcome you. Miss Percy mentioned it was close to Fernbank."

With the excuse of an unwanted lover ready to hand, Lucy did not hesitate to use it. She had not foreseen the plausible expectation that she should return to her own home. "Yes, and now you have the whole story," she said, hoping to put an end to the discussion.

"Not quite the whole," he countered. "There are a few details that still puzzle me. Would your family not protect you from an unwanted suitor?" He saw Lucy's frown, and found his own answer. "Or is it your family that press the match forward?"

"You ask a good many questions," she parried.

"I am interested to learn all about you," he said simply. The remark was accompanied by a steady gaze that unnerved her to no small extent. Avedon felt the swelling of pity and a desire to protect this woman, so recently considered an intractable foe, from all male advances, whether welcomed by her or not.

"It is a long story. I cannot think you would be interested to hear it." Yet she felt a strong desire to unburden the whole of it onto Avedon's chest.

"I am extremely interested," he persisted.

"Another time. This is hardly the place. We should be joining a square." She glanced to the floor, where sets were forming.

Avedon made no move to join the dancers. "Let me call on you tomorrow morning."

Lucy looked at him uncertainly. Why was it to this stern adversary that she wanted to tell her story and not to either of her more amusing and closer friends?

"Please let me come," he said, sensing her uncertainty, and consumed with curiosity to know her history, for he was now quite convinced she was not at all the kind of woman they had all believed.

"Very well," she said.

"I look forward to it. And I shall get a look at this whelp Morton has given you, too. Why didn't you tell me you wanted a dog? I have a new litter I want to be rid of."

"What a lot of unwanted creatures have come to disturb your peace this summer." Lucy laughed. "A pity you could not just give me away to someone, or drown me, as you probably will the puppies."

"I shan't drown them. They're valuable animals. Much better than Plimpton's. Sure you won't have one?"

She noticed he was minutely aware of her smallest doings, and smiled to herself. "One is sufficient. Puppies are liable to be jealous of each other, you know."

"I've noticed," he said playfully. "Morton and Tony are at each other's throats."

"You cannot call Mr. Carlton a puppy."

"You don't hesitate to call Tony one, eh? Poor devil, he's been run off by that hound of a Carlton."

"I didn't mean that! I am very fond of Tony."

"Is it a bitch Morton gave you? I have a male in my litter. Males are less trouble."

"That has not been my experience. And in any case, I am very fond of Sinbad. We call the puppy Sinbad."

"We do, do we? If he takes after his dame, Morton has given you a load of trouble."

"No, he takes after his papa. The same coloring, and such a lively nature. He teases the chickens to death."

"He wants a good thrashing."

"Morton says it ruins their disposition to be harsh on them."

"I see Morton has a deal of nonsense to say, as usual," Avedon charged, peevish to hear his cousin quoted as an authority.

Lucy stared to see him so angry at nothing. "You are a confirmed grouch, Lord Avedon. You cannot even discuss a puppy without losing your temper."

"I shall require a good many lessons to tame me," he said, and smiled to show her how eager he was to be tamed.

When the music resumed, it was a waltz that was played. Avedon drew her into his arms and they floated around the floor in a giddy whirl. It was like no dance Lucy had danced before. Ronald was just learning the waltz and performed it awkwardly. With Avedon it seemed to come naturally. Conversation ceased, and they gave themselves over to the reeling rhythm.

Lady Sara sat in a corner, watching her brother make a fool of himself over the waltzing widow, as all her other male relatives were doing. She decided it was time to enlarge the widow's circle of male acquaintances and looked around the hall for a likely candidate for presentation. She settled on Mr. Edgar, a successful merchant of Ashford, and sallied forth at the end of the music to make the two known to each other. She took Avedon's arm and drew him away while the other two chatted together.

"You shouldn't have presented Edgar to Mrs. Percy," Avedon said. "He is the very sort to take advantage of a woman in her circumstances."

"*Au contraire,* Adrian. He is the sort she ought to be taking advantage of. God knows there is nothing she prefers to traipsing through the village fingering the buttons and mauling the ribbons. A tradesman will do very well for her if she insists on having another husband. Or a husband, I ought to say, as she was very likely never married at all."

"Of course she was," he said gruffly.

"It was you who told me she was not! I know I told you to play up to her a little to make sure she doesn't trap Morton, but I hope you aren't going to be the next one requiring extrication from her clutches. Really I think the woman is part witch. She seems to bewitch everyone who gets near her."

"She is a charming lady."

"My dear, you have no idea how besotted you

111

looked dancing with her. Everyone was smirking to see you so easily gulled by a nobody. You must think of your position, Avedon. Would you really want that woman to rule at Chenely? Another man's leavings . . ."

Lady Sara let her eyes stray to the floor. She observed that Mr. Edgar, too, was smiling like a moonling. Perhaps Mrs. Percy had a supply of jokes that she used to entertain her partners. Lady Sara took the precaution of separating the parties from Milhaven and Chenely for dinner. She sat Lady Beatrice at Avedon's elbow, where she was largely ignored while her companion looked jealously across the hall to the table from Milhaven.

Chapter Ten

The next morning at breakfast Lady Sara received her reply from the Wesleys in Hampshire. A smile of triumphant astringency settled on her broad face as she read it.

"What have they to say?" Avedon asked.

"Just as we supposed," she answered, her bosom swelling with importance. "There was no Captain Percy killed at Ciudad Rodrigo. There was no Percy there as an *officer* at all. George Wesley knew them all, and there was no one there by that name. He does not even recall any noncommissioned Percy, and if the husband was only an enlisted man, you know, he was nobody."

Avedon set down his cup with a blank look on his face. "It's impossible," he said.

"There was an unmarried chap named Percy from Dorset in the Light Dragoons. He left his sweetheart at home and spoke of her often. George was there; he

113

would know. And anyway, he says nothing about that Percy being killed. She is a liar, as we always suspected. She heard of the Percys somehow—perhaps she is from the area, but she is not at all who she says she is. And I greatly fear, Adrian, that she has got Morton under her spell." She lifted her brows and nodded her head.

"But she is a lady! So well spoken and genteel."

"Genteel? Oh, my dear, you make me laugh out loud to hear you say such a thing. A pretty wench may do as she pleases with you men. Do but recall her having Tony hold her ice while she licked it—so vulgar, I nearly retched. And how well she got on with Mr. Edgar last night. Two limbs from the same tree, I swear. There is a little money there, I grant you. The establishment is well run, and she had on those diamonds. She might be a cit's daughter, looking for a leg up the social ladder. Or an actress . . ." Her voice trailed off as she mentally considered other possibilities.

Avedon listened critically. "I noticed she doesn't wear a wedding ring," he said.

"I didn't notice it! Well, that settles it. A grieving widow would not be in a hurry to remove the pledge of her husband's love." She looked at her own ring finger and smiled wanly. "I would not remove mine for worlds. Odd she didn't think of such an obvious thing as buying herself a gold band."

"I took another look at her letter applying for the house last night. It says quite definitely her husband *is* in the Peninsula. We thought the husband was supposed to be alive when she came here," Avedon said.

"She sat right there, bold as brass, and said, 'He is with Wellington,' or some such thing. She definitely indicated he was alive. She only decided to be a widow when she saw Tony, single and rich and ripe for plucking."

"But why did she come here in the first place, if she planned to pose as a wife and not a widow?" Avedon asked. "She could have had no thought of marrying at the time."

Lady Sara shook her head in repudiation of the whole affair. "What would I know about the schemes of lightskirts?" she asked, in a purely rhetorical spirit. "Perhaps her late *cher ami* was cutting up rusty."

Avedon considered this possibility and found it feasible. It seemed to jibe with all the facts. Mrs. Percy was hiding on a patron who had become obstreperous. She changed her name and marital status to make following her difficult, but once she discovered Tony, she decided to make herself available. A woman like that would be bored with no masculine company. The only thing that bothered him was why she had selected Tony for her new protector and not himself.

As he reviewed their relationship, it occurred to him that he had been antagonistic toward Mrs. Percy from the beginning. She had decided he was too farouche for her and settled for the young pup. After last night, however, she might quite possibly have changed her tune. It should be an interesting meeting. His first object was to get her away from the chaperon. Negotiations of the sort he had in mind didn't want an audience. He trusted she had enough town bronze to realize marriage was out of the question. In fact, as he considered it, he thought marriage had never been her intention. That would explain her refusal to move into Milhaven when Isabel invited her.

He rose and said, "I shan't be home for luncheon, Sal. I'm taking a run down to Seaview."

Lady Sara looked up with interest. Her papa had bought a seaside house at Shakespeare Cliff, near Dover, when she and Isabel and Adrian were young. The intention had been that they would spend some weeks of the summer there. Lady Avedon had taken the place in dislike and it was seldom used, except recently by Lady Sara and her family.

"Perhaps I'll come with you," she said uncertainly. "Are you thinking of opening it?"

"No, of renting it," he replied. "The place will be a shambles. It won't be very enjoyable for you, Sal. I'm taking my curricle to save time."

She envisaged the windy trip, a meeting with an estate agent, and perhaps a tour of the house, with no decent luncheon. "I shall stay home and ask Lady Beatrice to lunch," she decided.

Avedon breathed a sigh of relief and called for his carriage. On such a fine day the curricle would be pleasant. He knew Mrs. Percy had no objection to the open carriage, as he frequently saw her in Tony's.

Lucy had made a careful toilette in anticipation of his visit. She wore a fetching sprigged muslin with green ribbons and her curls were dressed *en corbeille*. She sat at her tambour frame, accompanied by her chaperon, when Avedon was announced. It always surprised him to find her at this domestic chore. For just a moment he felt a twinge of misgiving. What if he was wrong about her?

Then she looked up, and he saw the glint of mischief in her brown eyes. "I did not look for you so early, Lord Avedon," she said. "I made sure you would have estate duties to attend to before calling."

He bowed to the ladies. "I do occasionally abandon myself to pleasure," he assured her. "It would be a shame to waste a day like this working."

"I was thinking of taking my frame into the garden," Lucy said, "but the dust is still bothersome there."

"And the cow and chickens just a little closer to home than your nose finds comfortable, I wager," he added roguishly. "I hoped I might induce you to drive toward the coast with me. I want to inspect my summer house."

Lucy looked doubtfully at her chaperon. "We are expecting important company soon. I should help with the preparations."

"Your uncle does not come till the day after tomorrow. Run along," her aunt said. "It's such a fine day, and you always liked the sea, Lucy."

Lucy wasted no time in gathering up her bonnet and a pelisse, in case the sea breezes should prove chilly. Within minutes she and Avedon were cutting

117

along in his open carriage. He handled the ribbons of his blood horse with skill and precision. That jerking motion that made riding with Tony such a trial was totally absent.

"Where is your summer house, Lord Avedon?" she inquired.

"Not far from Dover. And incidentally, don't you think you might stop "lording" me. My name is Adrian, or if that is rushing things, at least call me Avedon."

Lucy was unsure whether an "Avedon" merited a "Lucy," and just nodded. "Are you preparing for a remove there for the summer?" she asked, and was aware of a sinking sensation inside her. Avedon had been a wretched nuisance, yet she knew the summer would lose much of its charm if he left.

He turned a practiced smile on her. "I hope to spend a good deal of time there. It has occurred to me that the sea air might be just the thing for you, Mrs. Percy. Perhaps you will honor me with a visit." She looked at him uncertainly, but he saw no real unwillingness in her attitude. "Miss Percy mentioned you are fond of the sea."

"Yes, I like it very much," she agreed readily

"I would hate to be parted from you, just when we are finally achieving a less quarrelsome footing," he said. "You must not think I am always so irritable as you have seen me."

"That would be difficult indeed," she replied with a saucy smile.

His answer was as close to flirtation as made no difference. "I think you know the reason."

"I haven't the faintest notion."

"Come now." He reached out with one hand and seized her fingers. "You aren't such a slow top as that. It was your pronounced preference for the other gents that got me on my high horse."

"And here I thought you feared I was angling after your nephew's fortune," she retorted.

Avedon released her fingers but held her with a smile. "Mine is considerably larger, you know," he said temptingly.

"If I were a fortune hunter, which I promise you I am not, that would count for a good deal with me."

"Then it is Tony's conversation that appeals to you," he said in a joking way. "By Jove, Mrs. Percy, I see I must step up m' compliments."

She smiled at his impersonation. "That won't be necessary, sir. It is his attitude that pleases me. He is always so eager to help, whereas some gentlemen go a mile out of their way to make my life miserable."

"And after all their effort they neither get their tiles laid, nor bounce off the unwanted tenant. Formerly unwanted tenant," he added, with a wider smile.

"May I conclude, then, that the war is over?" she asked.

"I have capitulated completely to my erstwhile enemy. You have taken the day, Mrs. Percy."

Lucy settled in comfortably, unaware of any ulterior motives in her host. "Did you really think I was interested in your nephew?" she asked

"Well, I knew he was interested in you. There is

something to be said for persistence, but I daresay a lady of your experience would prefer a—more mature gentleman."

"I think I would," she agreed. Lucy was still young and green enough to read his speech into a compliment. "There is also something to be said for worldliness. A more mature gentleman would not outsit his welcome so long."

The drive continued with good humor and flirtation on both sides. Lucy asked Avedon about his summer house, and he entered eagerly into a list of its merits. "We are close to Dover—I know you ladies like to be near the shops—but not perched on an impossible promontory. We have easy access to the sea for swimming and boating. I keep my yacht anchored there when I visit. Do you like sailing?"

"I've never sailed. We are not right on the sea in Dorset. Closer to Wiltshire actually."

"You will like it. The wind in your hair, the waves rolling under you, with the sun gleaming on the water. I hope you will agree to spend some time at Seaview."

"It sounds charming. When do you plan to go?"

"I wish we didn't have to go back home at all," was his oblique answer.

"I am promised to Milhaven this evening," she reminded him.

With Avedon's swift grays, the trip took only an hour and a half. They passed through the low-lying marshlands, with the terrain gently rising as they approached the coast. The scent of the sea, that salty mixture of iodine and seaweed, presaged the sea's appearance. Soon it came into view, a flat sheet of rumpled metallic motion, dotted with sails. He drew up in front of a rustic two-story building of flint and Caen stone. It was formed in the Norman fashion with rounded doorways, but the height and generous windows indicated it was of more modern construction. A puff of smoke rising from the chimney told her the place was not vacant. In front there was a patch of lawn, and wild roses climbed up the stone facade. Behind, a meadow of grass and wildflowers stretched in the distance.

"It's beautiful!" Lucy exclaimed.

"I thought you might like it," he said with quiet satisfaction. "Would you like to go and admire the sea before we go inside?"

She ran to the bluff, where a tumble of large rocks led to the sea. The wind whipped her hair and skirts. It also caused the water to swell, with whitecaps bouncing on the waves. "Nice and private for bathing," Avedon mentioned. "On a clear day you can see halfway to France."

"How lovely! You can take your yacht across the Channel," she said. A faraway look was in her eyes. She had an image of a halcyon future, with herself on Avedon's yacht, flitting across the water with the wind in her hair.

"We could gather up a group and have a race to Brighton," he tempted. "I think you would like Brighton, Mrs. Percy. I'm surprised you didn't choose to summer there. It is much livelier than our rustic little corner of the kingdom."

"I wanted peace and quiet," she said simply.

121

He put a hand on her arm and turned her back toward the house. "And I gave you noise and dust. What a shabby fellow. Let me offer you a quiet tea at least. I see by the chimney that my housekeeper is at home."

Avedon tapped at the door before entering. A local matron in a white apron and cap made them welcome.

"This is Mrs. Landry," he told Lucy. "I hope you can give us a cup of tea, Mrs. Landry, and perhaps some of your excellent bread or muffins."

"I have some buns in the oven this minute," she assured him. "The fire is laid in the grate if you're feeling chilly. I have only to set a light to it. There's always a nip in the air hereabouts."

"I'll light the fire," Avedon said, and led Lucy into the parlor.

While Avedon busied himself with the tinderbox, Lucy looked around the room. There was no real elegance here, but a cozy atmosphere, with the big stone fireplace occupying a whole wall. Around the grate ranged a fat stuffed sofa and two chairs. It was not a room for formal entertaining but a room for comfortable family living. Shelves of books and games ranged below the windows that gave a view of the sea. Sunlight slanting through the panes lightened the somberness of paneled walls. He lit the fire, and flames leapt up the chimney.

"This must certainly be a change from Chenely," Lucy said, looking all around.

"You don't care for so much rusticity?"

"It is charming, Avedon, for a little summer place."

Was she saying she had no intention of being satisfied with so little? Avedon felt a stirring of anger. "One would hardly expect to spend the whole year here, of course," he agreed.

"I expect it would be very cold in winter, and rather isolated, too."

"But wouldn't you prefer it to Rose Cottage—for the summer?" he asked.

Lucy looked at him in surprise. Was he inviting her to visit him for the entire summer? A flush colored her cheeks as she gazed into his brightly curious eyes. "I have just rented Rose Cottage," she reminded him.

"I would be happy to rent it back from you. There would be no expense in it for you."

"It's not the money. . . . It would seem odd to abandon it. Do—do you and Lady Sara intend to move here for the whole summer, Avedon?"

"Lady Sara?" he asked. "No, she will soon be returning to Hampshire."

Mrs. Landers brought tea, and Lucy poured for them. "Then it will be just yourself here?"

"You and myself, I hope," he said.

Lucy looked at him, with a smile trembling on her lips. She had always been aware of a tension between herself and Avedon. She knew that feeling was not all antipathy, but that it should turn to love in the twinkling of a bedpost was difficult to comprehend. "That sounds—rather—unusual," she said.

123

"There is nothing unusual in a gentleman falling head over ears in love with a beautiful lady," he said, and set her teacup aside to grab her two hands.

Lucy looked at him, blinking in astonishment. "This is so sudden, Avedon."

"Adrian," he said, gazing into her eyes and squeezing her hands till they ached. "And may I not call you Lucy?"

"I—I suppose that would be all right," she said primly.

He touched her nose and laughed. "Such a prim and proper little hoyden. This is not sudden at all. I have wanted to kiss you from the first moment I met you in the village, flashing your dark eyes at me and rattling me off for being a yahoo."

His head inclined to hers. Lucy was aware of a fierce thudding in her breast as the dazzle of his eyes came closer, blurring to a haze as she stared, hypnotized. His hand came to her shoulder. The other stole around her waist and he pulled her into his arms. She felt the solid, warm wall of his chest pressing against her as his arms tightened.

Her hands fluttered uncertainly a moment, then went around his neck. Lucy knew the treachery of allowing a man to embrace her. Even with the now-despised Ronald Pewter, she had felt these strange stirrings of passion. But Avedon was different. There was no reason to doubt his motives. He was a wealthy lord, and if he loved her, it had nothing to do with self-interest. She gave herself up to his embrace. His lips firmed as they clung together.

Strangely it was Avedon who brought the embrace

124

to an end. He wasn't surprised at the warmth of her response. He knew she was experienced; it was the depth of his own feelings that startled him. There had been more in the embrace than just desire. There was a strange new tender feeling. Perhaps it was the onset of love. It didn't do for a man to go falling in love with his mistress. That could lead to disastrous consequences. For the time being, however, he meant to forge ahead with his scheme.

Lucy looked at him, her eyes full of wonder, and smiled. "Well, that was a surprise," she said in confusion.

"Why, you were a married lady, Lucy. This cannot be new to you."

It was obviously the moment to inform him of the truth. Lucy girded herself for the telling and said, "I'm not exactly what you think."

He patted her hand in an avuncular manner. "There is no need to apologize, Lucy. I know more or less who and what you are."

"I was not going to apologize, exactly. Though perhaps I do owe you an explanation. Really I don't think you can know what I am, Adrian."

She was ready to admit all, but he was not in a mood to badger her for details. His smile was devastating as his eyes lingered on her face. "I know you are criminally beautiful, and I want to be with you. Now, let us set the date. When can you come to stay at Seaview? We must become better acquainted, Lucy."

Lucy took up her tea again. The "set the date" had confused her. She thought he was planning the wedding already, but it was a good idea to become better known to each other first. "I would have to consult with Miss Percy before I made any decision, of course."

"Yes, certainly I would prefer that she make other plans," he agreed.

"Other plans? Oh, she will stay with me till I am married at least," she exclaimed. Avedon gave a leap of surprise.

"That may be a long time. We wouldn't want her around," he said bluntly. "Naturally you would not want to be alone when I am at Chenely, but Mrs. Landers resides here. She would understand."

She frowned in confusion. There was obviously some misunderstanding afoot here. He could not be suggesting—"Understand what?" she asked.

"The nature of our liaison. I am offering you Seaview free of cost, as my guest for the summer months, with all a mistress's usual perquisites. Money, a clothing allowance. I would come to see you as often as my duties permit."

"Do you mean—are you saying—are you offering me a mistress-ship!" Fire blazed in her eyes, yet her voice was like ice.

Avedon allowed a tolerant smile of surprise to settle on his lips before speaking. "Certainly that was my meaning, madam. What else could I possibly want with a woman like you?"

Lucy had the strange feeling she was sinking into that cold, wind-tossed sea beyond the window. Avedon was calling her a lightskirt. He had never cared for her in the least. He had brought her for the specific purpose of insulting her. "A woman like you" he had said, as if she were a leper. It was shock that saved her. She wanted to dump her tea over his head, to revile and chastise him, and inform him her male relative would be calling on him to protect her honor. Except that one could hardly involve a bishop in a duel. So she sat silent a moment, thinking, listening to the thudding beats of her heart, while he stared at her with a contemptuous curl on his hateful lips.

And while she sat, it occurred to her that it would be extremely awkward to get home from this place alone. After this insult, she didn't doubt for a moment that he'd abandon her if she spurned his offer. Some cunning corner of her mind wanted to repay him in kind as well. What form this retribution would take was unclear, but he must be made to pay.

"You know me uncommonly well, sir," she said in a tightly controlled voice.

"I can see a pretty woman by daylight."

"I must give this my deepest consideration," she said, scanning possible revenges. One came to her in a flash. Why should *she* be the one stranded, unable to get home without great inconvenience? "And I really must tell Miss Percy. She oversees all my patrons," she added grimly. How to get rid of him for the necessary length of time? "Do you have to see anyone else while you're here, Adrian?"

"No, I just wanted to show you the house. Perhaps I should stop by Huddleston's place and tell him to prepare my yacht for the weekend."

"Oh, yes. We shall want to use the yacht," she said enthusiastically. "You must go to see him at once."

"You've hardly touched your tea."

"I can wait for you here. Is Huddleston's place very far?"

"It's just a few hundred yards farther along. He's a fisherman. He keeps my yacht for me. I'll walk over and be back in ten minutes."

"Don't be long," she said, batting her lashes flirtatiously.

Lucy steeled herself for the quick but ardent kiss he placed on her lips. It took all her fortitude not to attack him. He left, and the moment he was out the door, she ran out to the stable. She was relieved to see the team hadn't been unhitched. She hopped up in the driver's seat and wheeled the curricle out onto the road. The horses were already tired from their morning's drive, or she would never have been able to control them. It took all her strength to do it, but she was a good driver, and there was no need to spring them. There had been no other horseflesh in the stables. It would take Avedon a while to find she was gone and borrow or hire some other rig.

The task of controlling the high steppers occupied so much of attention that for the first half of the trip Lucy was unable to think of anything else. The occupants of other vehicles on the road turned and stared to see an unaccompanied lady wheeling along in a dashing yellow curricle. Her obvious gentility was all that saved her from jeers. By the time she was halfway home, the horses were becoming more fatigued and were easier to handle. She was very glad for it, as her fingers had raised blisters. Lucy was able to turn her mind to Avedon's insult.

What had possessed him to do it? It was a calculated insult, and to pretend he wanted to marry her was only done to humiliate her. Her heart burned like a red coal. She would never forgive him for this. Never.

The trip home took over two hours. Lucy was exhausted, dusty, and furious when she reached the door of Rose Cottage. She called the groom and told him to deliver Avedon's team to his stable with her compliments. She was not in a mood to give Mrs. Percy the necessary explanations, but her chaperon knew at a glance that something was amiss.

"What on earth happened, Lucy?" she asked.

"Avedon behaved abominably. I doubt we shall be hearing from him again."

"What did he do?"

Lucy burst into tears of frustration and ran upstairs, leaving the poor dame completely in the dark. A lover's quarrel, she decided, and didn't go after Lucy. She'd hear it all in good time. But in the near term all she heard was a message from the servant requesting that Miss Percy make their excuses for dinner at Milhaven.

Chapter Eleven

It was not till late afternoon that Lord Avedon arrived at Chenely astride a winded jade hired at the inn at Dover. His means of travel from Seaview to Dover had been even more degrading; it was a donkey cart borrowed from Huddleston. The opinion of such low people as Mrs. Landry and Huddleston mattered little to him, but still, he was livid to remember his embarrassment. He was in a temper that put Lucy's fit of sulks in the shade. His groom, familiar with this mood, did not ask any questions when he saw the black scowl his master wore.

"See that this moribund nag is returned to Fitchley's in Dover," Avedon said grimly, and tossed the reins of his mount to a groom. He saw from the corner of his eye that his curricle and grays were returned, and went to examine his team. They had been driven into the ground, but their mouths and legs appeared unharmed.

"When did these get back?" he demanded.

"Two hours ago. They was sent up from Rose Cottage," the groom replied. "Mrs. Percy sent her compliments with 'em, I believe."

"Thoughtful of her!" Avedon snarled. While he had plodded along in a donkey cart, Mrs. Percy had driven his rig. Someone would pay for this outrage. His fingers itched to connect violently with human flesh.

It chanced to be his sister who first encountered him inside the house.

"Adrian, what on earth happened to you?" she demanded, regarding his disheveled appearance.

"What does it look like?" he replied through thin lips.

"Are you digging up the meadow again?" she asked in confusion.

"What an excellent idea!"

He disappeared into his study. A bottle of brandy soon followed him in. He did not appear at dinner and sent word to the table that he was too busy to be disturbed. His body was sprawled on a chair, becoming slowly intoxicated, but his mind was active. Mrs. Percy had to be put in her place, and he was coming to realize that it would require a perfect plan to accomplish it. No maneuvering room must be permitted, or she'd weasel it to her advantage.

He thought of burning her house down and forbidding anyone in the neighborhood to take her in. But, of course, Isabel would be there with open arms to receive her and hand Tony over to the woman. He thought of calling the constable and having her arrested for stealing his grays—except that she had returned them unharmed. After a few more glasses of brandy, he suddenly found himself picturing her as his wife, under his cruel thumb till the day she died. He would lead her a sinner's existence in sackcloth and ashes. And even in sackcloth she would look irresistible enough to tempt the devil himself.

An immoral woman preying on youngsters should show some signs of dissipation on her face. She shouldn't have skin like rose petals, and unclouded eyes. He poured another glass of brandy and sipped slowly while bizarre scenes of love and hate reeled around in his brain.

Much later, but while he was still able to walk, Avedon went up to his bed. Evening had given way to night. Lady Sara had retired, and the house was in darkness. A glance at his watch told him it was midnight. He slept in his jacket and trousers. In the morning he awoke with a thundering headache and called for cold bathwater and a basin of hot water for shaving. After making a fresh toilette, he felt somewhat better but still unsettled as to how to handle Mrs. Percy.

His sister was at the table, awaiting her mail. "You look wretched today, Adrian," she said, scanning the smudges under his eyes. "I hope these bouts with the bottle are not a common occurrence, dear. Brandy is slow death. You have your duties to think of. Rattling off to Seaview with the widow may be your idea of handling her, but I must own, we all found it extremely odd."

"And how did we learn I took Mrs. Percy to Seaview?"

"Tony called on her. The chaperon told him. Lady Beatrice and I popped down to Milhaven in the afternoon to tell them what we had learned of the widow." As she spoke, she lavished butter and jam on a bun. "Isabel is such a peagoose, she lets Tony lead her by the nose. She did not censure him as strongly as one could wish, I fear. Tony planned to visit the widow the moment she returned. That wicked creature will get her talons into him yet if we do not get rid of her. What explanation did she give for feeding us such a parcel of lies?" She took a bit of her bun and chewed with relish.

"No explanation," he said. It did not till that moment occur to him that the subject had not even arisen.

"She hasn't a word to say for herself, eh? I trust she at least had the decency to offer to leave, now that her character is publicly known. At least she reneged on dinner at Milhaven. Tony dropped by last night and told me."

"I don't know what her plans are. She . . . left rather suddenly," he said. His face assumed an alarming shade of red at the memory.

Lady Sara sat down her bun and frowned. "How could she leave Seaview alone? Surely she did not take the common stage! Why, she would have to get to Dover first."

"No, she . . . found a carriage," Avedon said, for he could not trust himself to tell the truth without losing his temper and breaking all the dishes.

"I'm sure we are well within our rights to ask her to leave," Lady Sara said. "If she remains, we may

133

kiss Tony's fortune good-bye. It is obviously you, as the head of the house, who must do it, Avedon."

Avedon felt a strange reluctance to do anything of the sort. It would come down to a flaming argument, calling names, if Mrs. Percy even agreed to see him. She had the signed contract for the lease of the cottage, so he could hardly have a bailiff shove her out. Yet the woman must go. He decided the more rational chaperon was the one to talk to.

Lady Sara interrupted her eating to say, "You can tell her not a decent lady in the neighborhood will speak to her. I wonder if we might get the vicar to hint her away from church."

"A nice Christian attitude for a deacon's wife to take. I'll put it to Miss Percy."

"She ought to be exposed in the most public way imaginable as a lesson for other wayward girls. Brazen baggage. Her sort ought to be whipped at the cart's tail. She shan't get a penny of the five hundred back, either. You had the expense of using a dozen men to dig up the road. Let her rent pay for it."

"Try if you can control your greed and ill humor, Sally. I wonder where Miss Percy comes into all this. If *she* is an actress or an adventuress, I give up on my own judgment."

"I wonder . . ."

Avedon looked at her with interest. "What?"

"Is it possible she tricked Miss Percy into thinking she was married to the captain, to get herself a decent chaperon?"

"It cannot be that. His sister must know Captain Percy is alive. She could be the girl's mother—"

134

"That's who she is," Sally said. "The pair of them are wasting their time looking for a husband for the chit. They would do better to apply to Drury Lane. They are as fine a pair of actors as I have ever been privileged to witness. Oh, hurry, Adrian. I am dying to hear what she says."

Avedon rose immediately from the table but did not rush off to do his unpleasant duty. He dallied in his study for half an hour, thinking and pacing, till his sister came and hustled him out the door. All the way down the main road and up the access road to Rose Cottage he walked his horse at a slow pace, trying to explain Mrs. Percy's behavior in some rational manner. If she was a lightskirt, why had she spurned the advances of the richest man in the country? She told him she came here to get away from a man. Where did that fit into her story, or was it pure fabrication, to make him jealous?

She knew she had engaged his interest at the ball; he hadn't done much to conceal it. But it wasn't a lover she was after; it was a husband. She didn't display any reluctance when she had the temerity to think he was offering marriage.

At Rose Cottage Lucy knew the matter was not at an end. There had to be some reason why Avedon had insulted her. Someone had given him false information about her, led him to believe she was open to a proposition of that sort. Her reaction had shown him he was mistaken. He would come to apologize. As she wished to keep the whole mess under wraps, at least until after the bishop's visit, she hadn't told her chaperon what transpired at Seaview. A careful

135

consideration had led to the decision that she could spare Mrs. Percy at least that. Over breakfast she announced that it was time to let Avedon know the truth about them.

"I am relieved the acting is over," her aunt said. "They seem like good, decent people. It is a pity to deceive them, and for no real reason."

Lucy swallowed that description and said, "I never meant any harm. It was only to protect myself that I pretended to be married."

"When you decided you didn't want the protection of a husband, you shouldn't have made yourself into a widow."

"We had already written the letter. It was difficult to change."

Mrs. Percy did not think that any real harm had been done. She considered the matter to be a joke in questionable taste. "It will be interesting to see how things go on now. I doubt they'll be so busy pulling Bigelow away from you, when they hear who you really are."

"Oh, Tony—I don't think of him."

"Mr. Carlton has been taking over lately. He is pleasant, but he's too old for you, Lucy."

"He is only a friend, a companion to drive about with."

"Why is it Lord Avedon you have chosen to tell the truth to? That surprises me more than the rest, as you never cared for him." A pair of sharp eyes examined Lucy.

She looked away to hide her feelings. "He is Tony's guardian, the head of the house. . . . He is the proper person to tell, don't you think? If he calls, that is."

"I see. That's the only reason, is it?" Mrs. Percy asked with an arch look.

"Of course," Lucy replied loftily, and spoiled the effect by adding, "and don't think I like him, for I don't."

"How should you care for such a toplofty gentleman?" Her aunt smiled softly and rose. "He is neither too old nor too young in any case. This should be an interesting meeting."

"I am not at all sure he will call. He didn't say so."

Mrs. Percy left the room reluctantly and went on about her business. The bishop's bedroom had to be aired and cleaned. If he stayed more than a few days, she really should invite a few friends and neighbors in to meet him as well. But before any of this, she wished to tackle the mildew that was attacking the phlox.

Lucy was still at the table when the knock came at the front door. She recognized Avedon's voice, and heard with considerable curiosity that he asked to see not her, but her aunt. Now what was the plague of a man up to? She hastened into the hallway, wearing an angry scowl. "Miss Percy is busy. If you have something to say, you may say it to me, sir."

His bold eyes raked her from head to toe. "Very well. It concerns you in any case."

She led him into the parlor and closed the door. Her expression was not far from gloating when she considered what she had to tell him. Then he would see what a flaming jackass he had made of himself! "I trust you found your team in good order when you returned, Lord Avedon," she said boldly. "Sorry I couldn't wait to say good-bye, but there was just something about the atmosphere at Seaview that made me nauseous. The sea breezes, no doubt," she added ironically.

That she could make light of it was the last straw. An ill-concealed sneer took possession of his face. "Too much good clean air to suit one of your ilk, I expect."

"On the contrary, I found the air particularly foul, but then I am not accustomed to it, as you are."

"Just what rarefied atmosphere *are* you accustomed to, miss? Haymarket, perhaps? Yes, you may well stare. You have been found out."

Lucy turned a fiery eye on him. "I have nothing to hide. And I would like to know who told you I am a—a—"

"A Haymarket nun is the usual expression," he supplied. "No one told me. I have the use of my own common sense. There was no Captain Percy at Ciudad Rodrigo. Why claim to be what you are not? You are not a respectable widow but a lightskirt, come to try your well-worn charms on a credulous youngster. But by all means let me hear what you have to say. I am curious to learn who has been making a game of us all. The only thing I know for certain is that you are not a Percy."

His tone was almost as insulting as his words. Both combined were enough to jolt Lucy into fury. "You are mistaken, sir. I am."

"We have had a letter at Chenely from a neighbor of Lady Sara's in Hampshire. The son was with Wellington in the Peninsula. The letter stated that there was no Captain Percy at Ciudad Rodrigo, where your alleged husband is supposed to have met his death. You slipped up there. Captain Percy was engaged at Salamanca, not Ciudad Rodrigo, and he was not killed. You made a few other faux pas as well. You forgot to buy yourself a wedding band, miss."

Lucy's hand flew to her lips. How had she overlooked such an obvious thing? She saw Avedon looking at her naked finger, with a hateful grin on his face.

"Yes, really a remarkably stupid blunder on your part. Nearly as bad—no, *worse* than setting a butler at the door of a cottage. Bad ton, miss, but then, how should a woman of your sort know the customs of gentlefolk?"

"I am not accustomed to living in a cottage! At Fernbank we always had a butler," she charged angrily.

"I doubt you have ever been inside Fernbank, unless perhaps as a servant wench. Is that how you discovered the existence of Captain Percy? Did he used to squeeze you behind the doors?" His eyes ran over her figure in a blatantly assessing and insulting manner.

Lucy felt her blood turn hot at that examination. "No, sir, he kissed me in front of everyone, and I don't need *you* to tell me where he was stationed. Alex was killed in the battle of Salamanca the twenty-second of July at three in the afternoon, with a bullet through his heart. Would you care to see the letter from the Home Office informing me

139

of the fact? I have kept it by me as a memento. I have also a letter from his colonel commending his courage in battle, and several from his fellow officers."

She strode to a table and pulled out a wooden box. She removed from it a sheaf of paper done up in blue ribbon and thrust it at Avedon. He didn't even deign to glance at it.

"You're lying," he charged.

"Read the letters," she commanded, shoving them into his hands. He glanced at the one on top, which was indeed from the Home Office, addressed to Mr. Percy at Fernbank, announcing the death of Captain Percy at Salamanca.

"Where did you get this? What is the meaning of this?" he demanded angrily.

"What does it look like?" she blazed.

Avedon felt bewildered. He had finally convinced himself Lucy was a conscienceless adventuress and could not so swiftly make the adjustment. "But the letter from Hampshire said—"

"What do I care for a letter from Hampshire?" Lucy charged wildly. "Why should you believe the word of people you don't even know over mine?"

"But you told Sally it was Ciudad Rodrigo."

"I never said such a thing. Do you think it isn't etched into my mind where Alex was killed? You have the impudence to come here, implying I don't know him, whom I have loved since I could walk. You lure me off to that shack and have the effrontery to offer me a carte blanche, as though I were a—oh, it is monstrous!" She turned away, hot tears

140

scalding her eyes at all she had recently endured and the bitter memories the letters called up.

Avedon took a step after her but knew it was wiser to stop. He flipped through the other letters and saw that they were as she had said. He felt not only foolish but heartless, a beast. When he remembered his behavior at Seaview, shame was added to the rest. A sob escaped Lucy, and she put her two hands to her mouth to control it.

"Mrs. Percy, pray forgive me," Avedon said in a subdued voice. "I am grievously sorry." He glanced at the letters in his hand, wanting to put them from him. He laid them on the table and sought for a means of retreat. It was obvious that Lucy wished to be alone.

She was beyond words. A racking sob escaped her. He felt all the shame and remorse of a gentleman who has offended a blameless lady. "I am very sorry," he repeated. "It was a misunderstanding. Most unfortunate—unconscionable behavior on my part."

Lucy turned and faced him. Her face was wet from her tears, but her expression held more fury than grief. "I am not interested in your apologies or your offers, or your opinions, Lord Avedon. I don't know why you see fit to insult me and question every word I utter, to actually post letters around the countryside villifying my name, but when you question my relationship to Alex Percy, you go too far. Neither you nor any of the other gentlemen here are worthy to polish his boots, in spite of your fine titles and airs of self-consequence. To think I would be interested in a backdoor liaison with you, or marriage to that rattle of a Bigelow after knowing a man like Alex, a man who gave up everything for his country, for the likes of you—He left his home and family to face every danger. Oh, it is too much." She turned away, as if she could not bear to look at him.

"I'm sure he was a fine man," Avedon said. He felt helpless in the face of her tirade.

"Obliging of you to say so! The pity of it is that his sort are dead, while people like you remain at home to reap the rewards of his death and insult his family."

Avedon stood mute. The titled heads of families did not enlist to go to war, but it did seem unfair, even to him. "No reward is coming to me as a result of this unfortunate war," he said after a long silence.

"No, nor to anyone else." Her shoulders sagged, and she turned away, listless after her anger was spent. The aftermath of her outburst and her sad memories were with her still.

"I am very sorry for all the things I said to you," Avedon began, hoping to reestablish at least a speaking relationship. "They were totally uncalled for. They were unforgivable. I wish I could turn the clock back and unsay them. I hope, when you have considered the matter in tranquillity, that you will be kind enough to try to forgive me. I didn't mean to hurt you, Lucy."

Lucy glanced over her shoulder and was much struck with his humble posture and the beseeching light in his eyes. She remembered that she had still not told him the whole story. "This is all so foolish," she said distractedly.

Her remark seemed inappropriate. Avedon looked closely to see if she had recovered from the turmoil of their discussion. "It was indeed foolish of me," he said, to keep her calm.

"It's not entirely your fault."

This seemed more inappropriate yet. "You will want a glass of wine to calm your nerves," he suggested, and went to fetch it.

Mrs. Percy's curiosity had gotten the better of her and she went into the cottage to learn what was afoot. She heard Avedon go into the hall and went from the study to meet him. "Now you know the truth of us, what have you to say?" she asked roguishly.

"I am very sorry I had the impertinence to question your bona fides, ma'am. Mrs. Percy is very upset. May I have a glass of wine for her, please?"

"Certainly." Mrs. Percy's eyes started from their sockets at what she heard and saw. Mrs. Percy—so Lucy had decided against telling him the truth. She was on tiptoes to hear the story. "I'll take it to her," she said.

"That might be best. I'm afraid I upset her, talking about her husband. Will you be good enough to say good-bye for me, and tell her I am very sorry."

"I'll tell her," Mrs. Percy replied.

Avedon walked out the door into the bright sunshine, but he beheld nothing in the brilliant countryside to cheer him. He had never felt so ashamed in his life.

When Mrs. Percy took the wine to Lucy, she saw the tears on her cheeks. "What on earth happened?" she demanded.

"Oh, Auntie, it was awful! They have been writing around asking questions about us. They knew Captain Percy was not killed at Ciudad Rodrigo and thought we had made up the whole thing."

"That was my fault. I told Lady Sara Ciudad Rodrigo."

"And I told Tony it was Salamanca. When Avedon said I was no kin to the Percys, there was no standing it. I hardly remember what I said to him, but I was very angry. I showed him the letters Papa received from Spain," she said, nodding toward the letters that lay scattered on the table. "Of course he had to believe me then. Avedon was so polite through it all. . . ."

"You must tell him the truth, Lucy," her aunt advised.

"Yes. I was going to do it now, but he left. Why did he go? He said he would get me a glass of wine."

"I believe you frightened him off. Perhaps he'll return."

"Did he say so?" Lucy asked eagerly.

"He was too bewildered to think of it."

"Do you think he'll come?"

"Before you can say 'Jack Robinson.' He didn't want to leave but felt ashamed of himself."

Lucy gave a wan smile. "Now I feel ashamed. I should have told him the whole story when he was here, but he was so toplofty, there was no bearing it. Oh, why do men always have to be so impossible!"

"That's what I used to say till I met my husband." Mrs. Percy gave a conspiratorial smile.

Chapter Twelve

As Avedon rode home, he thought of the mull he had made of the whole affair. Offering a carte blanche to a respectable widow, hurling accusations at her. He had never been guilty of such terrible indiscretions before, and that Mrs. Percy should be his victim added salt to the wound. It was while he was stabling his mount that he recalled something Lucy had said before. She had mentioned a man she was escaping from. His blood simmered to consider that some scoundrel was trying to marry her, apparently with the connivance of her family in Dorset. He must do something to help with that intolerable situation. It would be a beginning to atone for his own crimes.

When he entered his house, he discovered that Lady Sara had gone to Milhaven, no doubt to inform them of his latest visit and pour more erroneous tales into the ears of the inhabitants. Was there no end to what Mrs. Percy must suffer at their hands? A memory of her tear-stained face and racking sobs rose up to bedevil him. He sent Sally a note telling her in a disjointed manner of their error and adjuring her to say nothing against Mrs. Percy. It was a long, soul-searching morning and half the afternoon before Lady Sara returned, her eyes large to hear the meaning of his cryptic message.

"Avedon, is this not the strangest thing? What have you discovered about them? Your note was such a scratched and blotched thing, I could not make head nor tail of it."

"I have incontrovertible proof that Mrs. Percy is exactly who she says she is. I never felt such a fool in my life. The only discrepancy is that her husband was killed at Salamanca, not Ciudad Rodrigo."

"Tony mentioned something of the sort when it came up at Milhaven yesterday. I was sure he had got it wrong." Her brow creased in concentration. After a moment she brightened and said, "Well, that explains it, then."

Avedon, watching her, wondered at her sudden change of mood. "There is nothing to smile at," he said testily.

"My dear, it is marvelous!"

"Marvelous, when I have just hurled every insult I could lay my tongue to at the woman?"

His sister gave a chiding look. "You cannot mean you have insulted that sweet child, Adrian!"

Avedon's voice was high in outraged disbelief. "It is more than half your doing!"

Lady Sara poured herself·a glass of Madeira and

prepared her speech. "I had a letter this morning from Mrs. Nivens, the widow of the late archdeacon."

"This is no time to start harping about that," Avedon snapped.

She gave one of her patient, forgiving smiles. "Wait till you hear what I have to say before you go flying off at the handle. So underbred, dear. You really ought to try to polish up your manners. Mrs. Nivens had been gossiping with Mrs. Wesley—just like them—they have nothing better to do than discuss every move I make. She, Mrs. Nivens, I mean, wrote me saying that the Percys from Dorset are closely related to Bishop Norris on the maternal side. Now, Bishop Norris, you know, has a great deal to say about the appointment John is seeking. The P.M. will certainly consult with Norris, and I have been at my wit's end to ingratiate him. I thought it the worst luck that Mrs. Percy was not who she said she was, for if she were, you see, and now we know she is—why, she is Bishop Norris's niece by marriage. And she is indeed the captain's widow! It is fate. No, it is God's doing. My prayers are answered, to send that wonderful, brave woman here, right when I need her."

Avedon stared at this about-face. "It was the work of Satan for me to lay into her as I just did."

"But what did you say to her, my dear?" she asked apprehensively. "I cannot believe you were abusive. There was no call for that. You are always a model of tact. I'm sure she was only a little displeased that we misunderstood the matter. . . ."

"More than a little," he told her bluntly. "You cannot go down there buttering her up. She hates the lot of us."

"Hate has no place in the Christian heart," she said piously. "The niece of a bishop must know that." Then she added in a more secular vein, "At any rate she don't hate Morton. He will turn her up sweet. I almost wish I could let him marry her. If Tony does not offer for Prissy, I shall."

Avedon shook his head at her delusions. "Come down to earth, Sal. Tony has no more intention of offering for her than I have."

"Do you really think so, dear? If I were to believe that, Morton might as well marry Mrs. Percy, for his money would only do us any good if he left it to Tony and Tony married Prissy. Otherwise it hardly matters. If Morton is to marry anyone, he could not do better than to get us connected to Bishop Norris. We shall just have to wait and see which way the cat jumps. I mean, which dear boy Mrs. Percy prefers, not that I mean to call her a cat. Imagine that sly Miss Percy not telling me she was related to the bishop when I mentioned him. Dear, I hope I didn't say anything to displease her and destroy John's chances. The archdeaconry is only the beginning of it. We might talk Norris into an early retirement, and John would be bishop before he is an old man. Why, we might even see him archbishop—it is all nepotism in these matters."

"You don't miss a trick, Sal. I'll say that for you, but you botched it up when you sent me down to Rose Cottage to make a fool of myself."

Lady Sara listened to him with an impassive countenance. "Did you mention my name?" she asked.

"I may have mentioned it was you who received the letter from the Wesleys," he said vaguely.

"Beast! Why must you go dragging my name into it? Not that she can blame me for what my neighbors say. And how is it possible Mrs. Wesley was wrong? Imagine that ninny of a Tony, knowing all along Captain Percy was killed at Salamanca and not telling us."

"Have you run out of people to blame?" Avedon asked, and in his state of distraction, he poured himself a glass of Madeira. One sip of the syrupy brew showed him his error. He gagged and set it aside.

"No, my dear, I know exactly whom to blame." She smiled a sly smile. "You. I shall have to blacken your character a little to bring the widow round my thumb, but you shan't mind that."

"No, indeed, why should I mind that? Feel free to denigrate me as much as you like if it will get John his appointment."

Lady Sara patted his fingers. "Don't sulk, Adrian. It is so unbecoming in a grown man. One step at a time. First I get on terms with her; then I have her here and let you ingratiate yourself—if you can manage it. Then we have the Percys invite Norris down here for me to work on. A dinner party, perhaps," she said in a musing way. "At least two courses and two removes, with all the best silver and china to impress him. Bishops are not above worldly considerations. I must discover from Mrs. Percy what meat he likes."

"Good luck," Avedon said, but his tone belied the kind words. He sat silent a moment, considering. "You told them at Milhaven that we were mistaken about Mrs. Percy?" he asked.

"I couldn't make head or tails of those few scrawling lines you sent me. I just slid the note into my reticule for you to decipher when I returned. As I had already had Mrs. Nivens's letter, however, I told them about the real Mrs. Percy's relationship to Norris."

"But they still believe Mrs. Percy is an impostor?"

"So I would assume. We must notify them at once. It would not do for Morton to jump in and revile her, too. We must save Morton."

"I'll go to Milhaven at once," Avedon said. He had no interest in saving Morton but was glad to have an excuse to do something. He really wanted to return to Rose Cottage but was too embarrassed to show his face.

"And I shall just slip down to Rose Cottage and see Mrs. Percy. Morton mentioned she liked dogs. I'll take her one of your pups."

"She doesn't want one," Avedon said over his shoulder. He was already at the door.

The trips to Rose Cottage and Milhaven both had to be postponed. The weather had worsened during the afternoon, and a storm was about to be unleashed on them. Black clouds gusted in. The wind tore at tree branches and whipped dust and debris along the ground.

"There is no danger of anyone from Milhaven striking out in this weather," Lady Sara said.

"No, and in any case, Mrs. Percy is so upset, I doubt she'd see them today."

"I cannot think they meant to go at all. Tony makes less than nothing of her being a lightskirt, but Morton is very cut up."

"What had he to say?"

"You know how satirical he can be when he chooses. He said he would give her a good piece of his mind and agreed with us that she should be whipped at the cart's tail. He also said a good many things about the muslin company that he should not have said in front of Isabel and myself. He was amazingly disturbed. I really think he meant to have Mrs. Percy. Perhaps he still does, as a *chère amie*."

Avedon paced the hall impatiently, occasionally opening the door to check the weather. The rain was pelting down hard now, slanting into the hallway. The storm promised to be a long one. Its first violence eventually subsided to a quieter but steady downpour. It was so dark that lamps had to be lit in the middle of the afternoon.

At dinnertime it was still raining steadily, and concern for getting to Milhaven was changed to concern for the roads being washed out and the crops drowned. By late evening the downpour petered out to a light sprinkling, but by then it was too late to go calling, and the unsettled business was shelved till morning.

Morton Carlton beat the storm to Rose Cottage by leaving as soon as Lady Sara departed from Milhaven. As he whipped his team along the road, his annoyance turned to mischievous pleasure. He enjoyed his bachelorhood, and while he was at that age where he wished to marry, he was not too old to enjoy one last fling with a pretty dasher. So, Avedon had been right all along, he mused. It was that prim and proper chaperon that had fooled him, but he had soon figured that out.

The dasher's present patron had shuffled her off to the country for some purpose of his own and didn't want her interfered with while away from him. The patron's wife had probably learned of the liaison and cut up stiff. If the patron was some well-inlaid duke or marquis, the dasher would very likely show a mere Mr. Carlton the door, but it was worth a try.

Mr. Carlton was told at Rose Cottage that Mrs. Percy was indisposed, but he thought he knew how to get past her defenses. He wrote a few lines and handed them to Higgs to deliver. Lucy read the note and smiled to herself. "Put me out of my misery. Is it true? As ever, Morton" was all he had written. It was enough to pique her interest. She had to discover what he had heard, and how.

When she appeared at the parlor door, her tears had long since fled. She wore a brightly curious eye and a tentative smile. "So you have come to have a look at the impostor," she chided.

Morton examined her closely and felt his opinion waver. "I have come to learn the truth of the bizarre rumors that are buzzing around you," he parried.

"So you shall," Lucy said. "There is no one I had rather tell." She was eager to have the truth known and relished the idea of Avedon hearing it second-hand. That would teach him to go flying off when he said he was getting her a glass of wine. "The story is a long one, so I shall call my chaperon," she added, and asked Higgs to call her.

"Well, Mrs. Percy?" Morton said archly.

"Actually Miss Percy," she corrected, and when her aunt arrived, Lucy explained the story from the beginning. She sensed that Morton was not entirely disposed to believe her, and showed him the letters she had shown Avedon. He examined them and shook his head, finally convinced.

"But why did you do such a thing?" he asked in confusion. "I can see posing as a wife to rid yourself of unwanted suitors, but why then transpose yourself into a widow? You take on the burden of a false identity with nothing to gain from it, no protection from the very sort of pestering you hope to avoid."

"Immediately after Mr. Pewter's attempt at my fortune, I took the decision to be a married lady to be rid of fortune hunters. I had begun to recover by the time I got here, and decided widowhood suited me better, as it offered some protection without making me totally ineligible," she explained, and went on to relate the gradual steps by which it had come about. He thought her a shatterbrain but no worse. And when he discovered the approximate size of her fortune, he found being a shatterbrain was entirely forgivable.

"So, Avedon and Sally have been sent flying into the boughs with this Banbury tale," he said, shaking his head.

"I meant to tell Avedon the truth, but he said such things to me—well, it is his own fault."

"Shall we keep the truth from him awhile, for a joke?" Morton suggested.

"No, indeed! I wish you would tell him at your earliest convenience." That would bring him running!

"I shall tell him at the first opportunity," he agreed, but he would take care no opportunity arose in the immediate future. He would just sit back and enjoy the confusion. It would be a good lesson to Avedon. Too toplofty by half, and it was clear as a pikestaff Miss Percy had tumbled for him. Let him simmer—and her too. "Will you come to Milhaven for lunch tomorrow?" he asked.

"It is tempting, but impossible. I am very busy tomorrow," Lucy said. "My uncle is coming to visit me. He has been attending an ecclesiastical meeting in London and will spend a few days here before returning to his diocese."

"Diocese?" Mr. Carlton asked with raised brow. "Then you are referring to a bishop." He didn't reveal by so much as a blink that Bishop Norris was of importance to his family.

"My uncle is a bishop," she replied proudly.

"What is his name?" Morton inquired quite unnecessarily.

"Bishop Norris," she answered calmly.

"Lady Sara's husband is one of his deacons," he said blandly, as though it were of little importance.

"My uncle is stopping at Canterbury. Aunt Percy and I had planned to meet him there and bring him here for a visit, but now—" Lucy came to an abrupt stop. She disliked to say that now she did not want to leave till Avedon came, and used her other excuse. "My aunt is a little fagged. She has been working like a Trojan in the garden. Uncle Norris knows she dislikes travel and will not be surprised if we fail to be there. He had wanted to show us around the cathedral."

"It is well worth the trip," Morton said with the keenest enthusiasm, and earned a rebukeful glare from the chaperon. "Have you seen the cathedral?"

"No. Uncle often speaks of it. We shall certainly go while we are in the neighborhood," Lucy replied.

"He is expecting us," Mrs. Percy reminded her. "We should send our own messenger if you don't plan to go, Lucy. There is no counting on the post to get a letter there in time. I daresay I can stand up to the trip if the weather is good. I don't like the looks of those clouds," she mentioned, glancing out at the lowering sky.

"Perhaps we shall go," Lucy said. She was confused and hurt that Avedon tarried so long in returning and wished to punish him.

Morton had some notion of how a lady's mind worked, and was all for egging her along. "If you are not looking forward to the trip," he said to the chaperon, "I will be happy to accompany Miss Percy. It happens I have business in Canterbury tomorrow and am going in any case." This was totally untrue, but a little mendacity never bothered him.

Lucy and Mrs. Percy exchanged questioning looks while each considered the desirability of this scheme.

Lucy imagined Lord Avedon arriving at the door and hearing she had gone to Canterbury with Mr. Carlton. That would show him she was not sitting cooling her heels while he vacillated. The chaperon's thoughts were equally selfish. She did not at all relish that long drive, and if she sent along one of her own trusted footmen, the bishop could find no fault with her guardianship. Mr. Carlton was a gentleman of unexceptionable breeding and reputation. He would certainly never do anything to jeopardize the reputation of a lady.

"You could return with your uncle," Miss Percy said encouragingly to her niece.

"Do come with me," Morton urged. "The trip will be a bore if I have to go alone. My team of bloods will get us there in two hours, just a nice outing."

"Very well," Lucy said.

"That is very kind of you, Mr. Carlton," Mrs. Percy added, with genuine feeling. "You must come to dinner while the bishop is here. We want to entertain him and have only a small circle of friends to call on as yet."

Morton rose and began making his bows. "You will have no trouble getting your noble neighbors to that dinner," he said, and laughed in a way that Mrs. Percy found peculiar till she remembered that Lady Sara's husband was a deacon. Perhaps the families were churchy. "Shall we say nine tomorrow morning, Lucy?"

"That's fine. I'll be looking forward to it."

"And now I shall rattle home before that storm breaks," Mr. Carlton said, and left.

The storm did not break for another half hour. Plenty of time for Avedon to call, but he did not. Lucy was irritable over dinner. A long afternoon dragged along endlessly, with the rain first streaming, then sliding down the windowpanes. Lucy spent half the evening at the window, monitoring the rain and the lighted windows of Chenely, visible up on the hill. It was only half a mile away. Why did he not come?

Mrs. Percy was more gainfully employed making up a list of invitations for the bishop's dinner party. Now that the whole truth was out, there was no problem about inviting anyone she wished. "Two from Chenely and three from Milhaven," she said to Lucy's back. "With ourselves and the bishop, that makes eight. I would like to have ten. The local vicar and his woman, perhaps . . ."

"We'll not invite anyone from Chenely," Lucy said mulishly.

Mrs. Percy's pencil hovered over the names, but she did not strike them off her list.

Chapter Thirteen

After passing a restless and troubled night, Lord Avedon was up at dawn, pacing the house and watching the clock's hands drag slowly toward ten, the earliest hour he felt he could decently call at Rose Cottage. At nine o'clock he thought nine-thirty was not too early, and at ten past nine he decided nine-fifteen was not straining the bounds of propriety. As it would take him more than five minutes to get there, he had his mount saddled up immediately and went ripping down the road. He avoided the meadow, as he did not wish to arrive splattered in mud.

It was twenty minutes after nine when he tapped on the door and waited. Higgs answered promptly and said affably, "Good morning, milord. That was quite a downpour we had last night."

"It certainly was. Is Mrs. Percy up yet, Higgs?"

"Hours ago." Higgs smiled.

"I would like to speak to her for a moment, if you please."

"I'm afraid you've missed her, milord. She drove off with Mr. Carlton."

Avedon's eyebrows drew together in a quick frown. "Mr. Carlton—at this hour?"

"Yes, milord."

"When will she be back?"

"Not soon. They've gone to Canterbury." Lord Avedon looked so stunned that Higgs added a word of explanation. "To meet the bishop," he said.

Driven off with Morton to Canterbury to meet a bishop—it suggested only one thing to Avedon. A special marriage license. "Are you sure?" he asked. As soon as the foolish question was out, he wished he could disown both it and the desperate voice in which it was spoken.

Strangely the question threw Higgs into doubt. There had been many unusual goings-on over the past weeks. Remembering to call Miss Percy Mrs. Percy, and vice versa. "It's what I was told, your lordship," he replied uncertainly.

"Yes, of course. Thank you."

Avedon left and went to his mount, which he had tethered in front of the house. With his mind in a state of chaos, he took the rein and walked down toward the road, trying to make sense of it. It was soon pitifully clear. Lucy had accepted an offer from Morton. They were in such a rush to be married that they could not wait for the banns to be called. They had gone to the bishop for a license. Archbishop it would be, if they went to Canterbury. Odd Lucy hadn't applied to Norris, but Canterbury was closer, of course.

He rubbed his jaw. He had read something in the journals recently about Archbishop Manners-Sutton being at his Lambeth Palace seat in London—some episcopal conference. Perhaps one of his diocesan bishops was handling cathedral affairs. Despondency sat like a cloak on his shoulders. He felt as if the sun had fallen into the sea, and he would never see it again. Lucy married to Morton. It was infamous. He wouldn't allow it.

When he realized what folly his mind was wandering into, he clenched his jaw and pulled himself back to reality. He was curious to learn all the details of the match, and the place to do it was obviously Milhaven. He clambered onto his mount and dug his heels in till the great gelding was galloping down the road. Trees and houses and fields of cattle rushed past unseen. In his mind Avedon was wildly contriving some means by which he could oust Morton in Lucy's affections in the short few days he had left.

How had he been so insane as to let Morton win her? Why had he not come down off his high horse and told her he loved her? He had sensed that she had some interest in him from the first meeting. Oh, nothing obvious, she was too proud for that. But there had been a tension when they were together, a quickening of the air, a hastier beating of the heart. A man knew when a lady was interested in him. And what had he done to fan this flame? He had followed his first cool reception on the High Street by making her life a living hell. He had torn up her road, offered her a carte blanche, gone into her home reviling and chastising her. And to add the final, infamous insult, he had called her a liar and a conniver. Good God, he'd be fortunate if Morton didn't demand satisfaction.

Before long the brick walls of Milhaven appeared, and he put his mount over a fence, angling across a meadow to shorten his path. He didn't bother knocking on the door but just flung it open and pounced in. Tony was sitting in the saloon with his legs stretched out straight in front of him. He was dressed for riding, in buckskins and topboots, and held a crop, which he occasionally tapped on the floor while waiting for his mount to be ready.

"Avedon, what the deuce brings you here?" he demanded, looking up in surprise. His pale face wore a sulky expression.

"I came to discover what you can tell me about Morton and Mrs. Percy," he answered.

"He's gone to Canterbury on business," Tony replied in a dull way. "You need not fear she's trapped him, Uncle. Aunt Sal told us all about her. Morton was out of reason cross. I'm sure if Lucy was letting on she was married to Captain Percy, there is some good reason for it."

"There is no call to take that condescending tone. She *was* married to him," Avedon said sharply.

"Aunt Sal told us it was all a hum."

"We were mistaken." A feeling of disquiet grew in Avedon.

"I knew it all along," Bigelow declared triumphantly. "Haven't I been telling you you misjudged Mrs. Percy?" He paused a moment and added with a sly look. "But Morton don't know about it, and he's jaunted off to Canterbury." He rose and began straightening his jacket. "Do you know, Uncle, it's such a jolly fine day that I'm going out for a ride. Perhaps to the village," he added, for he wished to get to Rose Cottage unaccompanied, to resume the flirtation before Morton returned.

Undeceived, his uncle said, "She's not at home. She went to Canterbury with Morton."

"He wouldn't have invited her," Bigelow said. "He had some pretty sharp things to say about Lucy."

Avedon's feeling of disquiet began swelling to anxiety. "I tell you, she went with him. I've been at Rose Cottage." He drew a long breath and announced, "Higgs told me they'd gone to get a marriage license."

"Rubbish! Marriage is the last thing he had in his mind." They exchanged a look of dawning suspicion. "Good God!" Bigelow exclaimed. "You don't think he's—no, it cannot be an abduction. Her chaperon must be with them. She wasn't at Rose Cottage, was she?"

"I didn't see her. If Morton isn't arranging a wedding—well, it is pretty clear what he *does* have in mind." Avedon strode purposefully toward the door.

"Wait for me!" Bigelow shouted, and ran after him. There was a nervous delay while Bigelow's mount was brought around to the front. "I'm just going to take a nip up to Morton's room and see if he left us a note."

"He's not a runaway schoolboy," Avedon said, but Tony ran off.

When he returned he announced, "If he was getting married, he would have worn his best jacket. He didn't. It's hanging in the closet. And furthermore, he didn't take his prayer book with him."

"He doesn't need his best jacket to get a license," Avedon pointed out.

"He has no intention of marrying her. He's seducing her."

This possibility was enough to fire both gentlemen to a new pitch of wrath against Morton Carlton. "I know just when he hatched this whole scheme," Bigelow said through thin lips. "As soon as Sal left yesterday afternoon, he had that old mare of his saddled up and went posting off. That's when he went to Rose Cottage and fed Lucy this Banbury tale about getting a marriage license. That was to con her into going off with him."

"Perhaps she convinced him of the truth," Avedon said uncertainly.

"Why didn't he tell us last night, then, when he returned from Rose Cottage? Not a word did he say, but only sat there grinning like a jackal. Now we know why."

Avedon listened intently. "We'll stop at Rose Cottage and see if Miss Percy went with them," he decided.

"And if she did?"

Avedon came to a frowning pause. Morton was not a savage after all. If Miss Percy was with them, then the affair was respectable, and it would be obtrusive for him to go pelting after them. When he finally spoke, it was not about Miss Percy. "I wonder what time they left," he said.

"He was gone before I came down. We'll ask Higgs."

They knew even before they reached Rose Cottage that Miss Percy had not accompanied her charge. Through the trees along the side of the road they caught a glimpse of her sunbonnet in the back garden. Avedon disliked to throw the poor soul into alarm. He rode around to the rear and worded his query discreetly.

"Good morning, ma'am," he said, trying to force a smile. "I hear your charge has gone to Canterbury."

"Oh, good morning, Lord Avedon—Tony. Yes, she has gone off with Mr. Carlton—to meet the bishop, you know. Higgs told me you were here earlier." She assumed Carlton had told the family the true story by now.

"Yes, at what time did they leave?"

"They wanted an early start. They left around nine."

Avedon pulled out his watch. It was a few minutes past ten. God, they'd never overtake them. "Thank you," he said, and turned his mount around.

Mrs. Percy smiled softly to herself. Avedon wasn't too happy about that. Very likely Lucy had only accepted Carlton's escort to rouse a little jealousy. She expected to see Avedon again before sunset.

164

"How fast can that jade move?" Avedon asked his nephew.

"Jade? I'll have you know my blood can outrun anything on four legs. She can go fast enough to beat Carlton's tired old hacks to Canterbury, even with an hour's lead."

They both dug in their heels and galloped down the road to Canterbury, while mud from last night's downpour splattered in all directions. Their pace left little time for conversation but did not stop their wild imaginings of Lucy at the mercy of an accomplished womanizer. To that extent their imaginations rode in tandem. From there Tony's veered off into wild and unlikely rescue scenes involving swords and guns, neither of which he or Mr. Carlton carried with them.

Avedon's daydreams were hardly more realistic, except that they involved fists. He wanted the satisfaction of physically pummeling Carlton's handsome face with his own fists, after which a grateful and repentant Lucy would throw herself on his bosom. As the miles flew by, more practical considerations rose up to disturb his fantasies. He should have told Sal or someone where he was going. Tony hadn't left any message, either.

After the first unrestrained gallop, they had to slow the pace for the horses' sake, and conversation was possible. "What if it ain't Canterbury they're headed to at all?" Bigelow asked. "It could be a ruse, Uncle."

"He told her Canterbury. He'd have to head in that direction, or she'd suspect something amiss. We know it isn't Gretna Green in any case, for you don't need a special license there. I should think it is marriage. They definitely went to see a bishop, according to Miss Percy."

"He might think she was bamming him." But no more likely destination occurred to Bigelow, and he accepted his uncle's word. "Where in Canterbury do you think they'd go?"

Avedon had no more idea than his nephew. "We'll drive down the High Street, check out the inns, the banks of the Stour, the area around the cathedral," he replied, as these were where tourists might expect to be found.

"Shouldn't we go to the cathedral first?"

"If they're at the cathedral, then Lucy isn't in danger. They're getting a marriage license. It's the inns we have to worry about." It occurred to him that this was a highly unsatisfactory plan. They weren't even sure Canterbury was their destination.

"We'd make better time if we split up," Bigelow suggested. "But we'll need a meeting place. How about the Rose, in High Street? That is where Papa always stayed."

"That's as good as any."

"We'll go there first and hire fresh nags. I hope you brought plenty of blunt, Uncle, for I meant to go to the bank today. My purse is as flat as a spinster's bosom."

"An edifying simile. I can afford a room and a nag at least."

"We'll hire the room first. I wish I had brought a change of shirt and cravat with me. We shall look like a pair of ruffians, going after Carlton with the dust of twenty miles on us."

Avedon spared a glance for his companion and realized that he must look as bad himself. It was not dust that splattered them both from head to toe but mud. Every carriage they passed, and they passed many on this well-traveled thoroughfare, left its traces on their buckskins and boots. In low-lying areas where water stood in puddles, the splatters reached up to their jackets.

"Damme, I wish I had driven my curricle," Bigelow said a few times. "Carlton will look as fine as ninepence. Lucy will be ashamed to know us."

These were minor irritations, but together with the more serious problem of finding and rescuing Lucy (if necessary), they made for a thoroughly miserable ride. The riders were as fagged and as dirty as the horses by the time they entered the city. Bigelow insisted on hiring a room and repairing his toilette before continuing on his quest. Avedon waited only to get a fresh mount before beginning a systematic search.

"Don't be too long about this cleaning up," Avedon said. "I'll check the inns on High Street. You take Palace Street and Burgate. We'll meet back here when we've finished."

"I shan't be two minutes," Tony assured him.

Avedon found it a depressing business, going from place to place and always hearing the same answer. No one matching Carlton's and Mrs. Percy's descriptions had checked in.

He realized he should have brought a dozen servants with him to assist in the search. It was by this time well after noon. He was tired, dirty, hungry, dispirited, angry with himself and Lucy, and more anxious then ever to find her. Hoping Tony had had better luck, he repaired to the Rose. He found his nephew enjoying a leisurely luncheon in a private parlor, looking as good as the inn's valet could make him. He had got hold of a clean cravat and had the filth of travel brushed from him.

"By Jove, Avedon, you look like something the cat dragged in," he said. "I'll order you a beefsteak while you wash your face and comb your hair. You don't want Lucy to see you looking like a scarecrow."

"Did you have any luck?" Avedon said, and sat down with a weary sigh.

"Eh?"

"I've done the inns on High Street. Did you check the ones along Burgate and Palace Streets?" he asked impatiently.

"Not yet."

"When did you plan to start?" Avedon howled.

"Damme, I could hardly eat a bite of breakfast. I was famished, if you want the truth. And besides, I don't think he even brought her to Canterbury. I mean, if you was abducting a woman, Avedon, would you tell her chaperon where you was taking her? Devil a bit of it. You'd head off in the other direction. I daresay they're halfway to London by now, while we make fools of ourselves looking for them in Canterbury."

Avedon tried to ignore Tony's harping on seduction, but if Lucy had not convinced him of the truth,

168

it was just such a stunt as Morton would try, to repay her. Frustration grew till he could hold it in no longer. "Why the hell did you bother coming, then, if you only mean to recline at your ease, swilling ale and stuffing your face?"

Bigelow gave one of his sulky looks. "You convinced me at the time, but now I've thought it over, I realize we ran off half-cocked. Have a glass of ale, Uncle. You'll feel better."

Avedon took his nephew's glass and drained it. The cool, bitter brew felt good against his burning throat. He set down the glass and said, "Since we're here, we might as well check out the cathedral. That's where they said they were going."

"That's exactly where they won't be, then," Bigelow replied. "And anyway, you can't go into a cathedral looking like a pilgrim."

"Don't display your ignorance. Pilgrims and the cathedral have a long association." He took a piece of bread from Bigelow's plate and ate it as he returned to his mount.

He felt, in his bones, that it was futile to continue searching in this city, but decided just to try the cathedral, then return to the inn and take lunch. Like Tony, he had eaten little breakfast and was feeling the want of food. As he approached the cathedral, he saw masses of well-dressed tourists and felt all the shame of being so disheveled himself.

As he stood looking about for Carlton's carriage in the churchyard, he heard the cathedral bells ring out. Their joyful peal told him it was not a funeral. Was it a saint's feast day—or perhaps a wedding? A tremor ran up his spine. No, Miss Percy would be with them if it were a wedding. If they were here, it was for a license. He walked on past a pretty Elizabethan-fronted house, which someone had told him was the Deanery, where distinguished guests sometimes stayed—perhaps even Lucy's uncle Norris, the bishop. A frown pleated his brow. Was it possible the bishop was visiting Canterbury? Could that be the bishop she was going to see? If Carlton knew she had an uncle who was bishop, he would realize she was no lightskirt, but a true lady.

As he glanced at the Deanery, he saw a black carriage parked in the shade of a spreading elm. It looked like Carlton's. He hastened forward and confirmed that it was. The joyful wedding bells pealed from the tower. Wisps of fact and possibilities reeled around in his mind. Lucy, Morton, gone to see the bishop—and wedding bells. Had they come to be married, and Lucy kept it hidden from her chaperon? It seemed pointless. Morton was an entirely eligible suitor, and not of an age to be making an adolescent runaway match. But the awful possibility remained that they had been married while he futilely racketed around from inn to inn, thinking to rescue her.

Chapter Fourteen

Lucy's trip to Canterbury was much less harrowing. In a well-sprung chaise and with a charming companion to beguile the hours, she had no greater weight on her mind than that she would not be at home if Avedon called. She took some petty pleasure from considering his surprise when he learned she was away for the day with Morton. They drove directly to the Deanery, where her uncle stayed when he was at Canterbury.

"Come in and meet my uncle, Morton," she invited. "He will give us luncheon."

Morton knew his duty and was happy for the opportunity to butter up this potential benefactor of Dr. Rutledge.

Bishop Norris was cheered to see his niece in such improved spirits. "How are you, my dear?" he asked, and put his arms around her. "And where is our Mrs. Percy?"

"You know how she dislikes travel, Uncle. Mr. Carlton was coming to Canterbury on business, and was kind enough to deliver me and let her stay home. She is busy bringing order to the chaos of an abandoned garden. I would like you to meet Mr. Carlton. He is visiting my landlord, Lord Bigelow. They are cousins."

Such close kinship to the nobility was taken as prima facie evidence of good character, and Mr. Carlton was greeted with warmth. The bishop thought Lucy had found herself a new beau and was happy for her. The lad was a little long in the tooth but by no means an antique. Of course his character and financial condition must be looked into closely.

"I daresay you are both ready for a bite," he said. I'll just tell Mrs. Stapleton to lay another plate. Bishop Redding came as far as Canterbury in my carriage with me, but he has continued on his way. There will just be the three of us."

Mr. Carlton graciously accepted and put the luncheon to good use. Before long, the name of Lord Avedon joined that of Lord Bigelow in his conversation. "I have the pleasure of his sister's company," the bishop said. "She is married to one of our deacons in Hampshire, Dr. Rutledge. We have lost our archdeacon there and must appoint a new man. Our problem is one of too many fine candidates. They are all good men."

Mr. Carlton was too cagey to push his own candidate forward at this time. That would be for Sal to do more cleverly when she entertained him. "Lady Sara is at Chenely now," he said. "I'm sure she will be delighted to hear you are visiting your niece."

"She has often asked me to visit Chenely when I am in the neighborhood. I must stop by and say how do you do," the bishop said. "Is Dr. Rutledge with her?"

"Oh, no. He would not forsake his ecclesiastical duties for so long," Mr.Carlton replied cagily. "Lady Sara usually stays a month. The family is very close."

The bishop nodded, untouched by the deacon's rectitude. "I expect he has his hands pretty full, with our archdeacon gone. The more so if his wife is also away."

The conversation turned to other topics, and Mr. Carlton made no effort to prevent it. After lunch he prepared to take his leave, claiming a few business matters to attend to. "I leave you in good hands, Miss Percy," he said with a smile at Lucy and a bow to the bishop.

"When will you be returning to Milhaven?" she asked.

"Today. My business won't take me long."

"I shan't invite you to call till tomorrow," Lucy said. "My uncle will be tired this evening after the trip. Shall I look for you tomorrow?"

"Certainly. Lord Bigelow and his mother will also wish to pay their respects to Bishop Norris," he added with another bow to the uncle.

"Don't get up, Uncle," Lucy said when the bishop began to rise. "I'll see Mr. Carlton to the door."

In the hallway she turned a laughing eye on Morton. "I know what you are up to, sir!" she charged. "You hope to land that promotion for Dr. Rutledge.

My uncle is not at all susceptible to titles, you know."

"Let us hope he is susceptible to the flattery of noble matrons, then. He'll have the silver butter boat dumped on him at Chenely, if I know Sal."

"Is Rutledge a good man for the job?" she asked. It pleased her to have some slight sway over Avedon's sister.

"He knows his Bible by heart. A quotation leaps out of his mouth every time he opens it. He is obviously a saint; he's lived with Sally for two decades without strangling her. Whether that makes him a good candidate is not for me to decide. He'll do as well as the next man, I expect."

They were at the door. "Thank you for bringing me, Morton. I had a lovely time."

"It was my pleasure," he said with a gallant bow.

They said their farewells, and he went out to his carriage. As the groom held the door for him, Lucy stepped out to the porch to wave good-bye. From the corner of her eye she noticed a dark and ill-kempt form loitering across the yard. He began stalking forward in a purposeful manner. She felt a little spurt of alarm, looked again, and recognized Lord Avedon, looking as if he had just crawled out of a dustbin. She and Morton exchanged a questioning look, and each advanced toward the other, meeting at the end of the walk leading into the Deanery.

Avedon continued toward them at a stiff-legged gait. What could he be doing here? He looked so wild-eyed and angry that Lucy could not imagine what had happened to him. Morton followed her gaze and had to quell down a burst of laughter. It did not occur to him that he was about to be accused of marriage, but he knew Avedon well enough to know that he was in a great pelter about something, and nothing seemed more likely than jealousy.

"Cousin," he said with a bow. "If Sal has sent you here to try your hand at cajoling Bishop Norris, I suggest you take a brush to your jacket before calling."

"I am not here to see the bishop," Avedon replied with a sneer. "I leave that to you two." He turned a menacing face to Lucy. "This was very sudden, was it not?"

She stared in confusion. "Not in the least. The trip has been planned for some days."

"You've kept your plans very close to your chest. But then, that is nothing new for *you*."

"I don't see that it's any of your concern," she answered hotly.

"You might have told me."

She lifted her chin haughtily. "I might, had I thought it any of your business."

He clenched his jaws and asked in a hoarse voice, "Is it already done?"

Lucy looked to Mr. Carlton in confusion, then back at Avedon. "We have already met my uncle."

His words lashed like a whip, and sparks shot from the banked fires in his eyes. "I mean the clandestine wedding."

She stared a moment, shocked into silence. "There was no clandestine wedding. And if there were, I should like to know what you are about, lurking outside the door like a hedge bird in that filthy jacket

175

to make a mockery of it. I suggest you return to Chenely and devise some other ruse to make my stay at Rose Cottage untenable. Hire a pack of Gypsies to camp in the garden. Set up an abbatoir. You are not at all imaginative, milord."

"Are you married yet?" he demanded.

Lucy turned abruptly away from him. "Pray take your cousin away, Morton, before the housekeeper has the dog set on him." She turned back to Avedon. "Not that you don't deserve it!" she added.

"You'd best run along, Avedon," Mr. Carlton said, biting back a grin to see his stiff-rumped cousin so disgraced.

Avedon felt, for the first time in his life, the degradation of being turned off, and to complete his humiliation, it was done publicly, in front of a friend and relative. His whole family would hear the story before nightfall. After his long day's worry and exertion, this was enough to finish him. The last vestige of common sense fled when he saw Carlton's smirking grin. "Who's going to make me?" he asked in a challenging voice.

"Avedon, for God's sake!" Carlton laughed.

"What's the matter, Carlton?" he taunted. A blood lust had risen up in him. If he didn't hit someone, his head would burst open. It felt swollen, like an inflamed tooth, throbbing, aching

Carlton looked a question at Lucy. "He must be foxed," he said in confusion. This was not the Lord Avedon he had so long known and admired. "Do run along, Avedon."

"I'm as sober as you are," Avedon replied. He

176

dared not look at Lucy. She must think him a yahoo. Yet he couldn't stop. He was like a charging horse, run out of control. "Well, Carlton? I repeat, who's going to make me?"

Carlton's lips lifted in a quiet, anticipatory smile. "This isn't the time or place for a match, Avedon, but if you'd care to step into my carriage, I'll be happy to oblige you elsewhere."

"Here, and now. You ordered me to leave. I'm staying."

"You leave me no alternative, old chap," Carlton said, and raised his fists. "You'd best step inside, Lucy," he said over his shoulder.

Lucy, of course, stayed rooted to the spot, her eyes gazing in disbelief. "I wouldn't miss this for the world," she said. "I have wanted to see someone teach Lord Avedon some manners from the first time I met him."

Avedon raised his fists and landed Mr. Carlton a facer. Carlton was caught off guard, for he still couldn't quite believe that Avedon meant to indulge in a fist fight on the grounds of Canterbury Cathedral. He went reeling back, tripped over an edge of cobbled walk, and landed in the dust.

Inside the Deanery, Bishop Norris was eager to show Lucy her tour of the cathedral so that they might get home before dark. He decided to join her and went for his hat. As he opened the front door, he saw an uncouth lout raising his fists and menacing Mr. Carlton. Even as he looked, the lout struck out, and poor Mr. Carlton went reeling back onto the ground.

177

The bishop raised his cane and advanced, shouting at Avedon. "Out, cur. Have you no respect for God or man, to institute a quarrel in this hallowed spot!"

For one awful instant Lucy feared her uncle was about to receive a blow on his chin. There was fire in Avedon's eyes as he turned. But when he saw the gentleman's age and clerical garb, he was jolted back to propriety. He cast a frustrated glare at Lucy. She was as white as paper and looked frozen.

The bishop continued his verbal attack. "You ought to be ashamed of yourself, sir. I have heard of you bucks beating up the watch and terrorizing decent people by overturning their carriages, but this beats all the rest, to attack an innocent man in this holy place. Flogging is too good for you. Lucy, fetch a footman and send him off for a constable. This jackanapes will spend the night in the roundhouse."

Lucy still stood, transfixed. It was Mr. Carlton who averted disaster. "It's quite all right, milord," he said, struggling to his feet. "A misunderstanding. This . . . gentleman is an acquaintance of mine. A little the worse for wine," he invented. "I'll take him off and sober him up. I am devastated that this should happen on your doorstep. My humblest apologies."

"You ought to choose your friends more carefully, Mr. Carlton," the bishop said, but leniently. "Come inside, Lucy. You look like death." They went inside, and Carlton led a shaken and contrite Lord Avedon to his carriage.

Once they were safely concealed inside, Mr. Carlton could no long contain his mirth. He laid his head back and laughed till his eyes ran tears. "Oh, Avedon, this is worth a quarter's allowance, to see you make such a cake of yourself," he gasped. "What on earth were you thinking of?"

Avedon sank his head in his crossed arms and groaned. "Oh, God, I must have been mad."

"Completely deranged," Morton agreed, "but it's a pity this fit descended on you in front of Bishop Norris. He plans to call on you at Chenely." Another spurt of uncontrollable laughter erupted from Carlton's throat.

"Let us drive away," Avedon said grimly. Lucy and the bishop had already entered the house, but he feared they might be looking out the window.

"Where can I take you?"

"What does it matter? I am ruined. What must she think of me, Morton?"

"Lucy, or Sally?"

Carlton decided that only unrequited love could cause the pain and grief he read in Avedon's eyes. He pulled the check string and the carriage drove off, heading for High Street.

"Go to the Rose," Avedon said in a dull voice. "I am to meet Tony there. I'll have to send someone after my mount. I left it tethered near the cathedral."

"Good God, did you have the lack of sense to bring that cawker of a Tony along with you? Why did the two of you come here to Canterbury?"

"Why do you think? We learned at Rose Cottage

179

that you and Lucy had gone to see the bishop. We thought you planned a hasty wedding," he said, suppressing his worse fear.

"This sounds like a very extreme case of puppy love, old boy. Not an appetizing sight in one of your years. How could you be such a flat? Did you seriously think we had darted off for a quick wedding? What would be the point of it? Or of your coming hell-for-leather after us, for that matter? We are both of legal age."

Avedon rubbed his jaw and tried to salvage some shred of self-respect from the debacle. "Tony convinced me you had run off with the widow. After Sal told that wretched story about her . . . When did you learn the truth?"

"Last night."

Avedon scowled at this evidence of intimacy. "Odd you didn't mention it at Milhaven. Not knowing that you knew the truth, Tony thought it was not a wedding license you were after, you know, but something else."

"No more it was a wedding—nor an abduction, either, if that is what you are implying. I'm highly flattered, of course, that you should believe me so dashing. I merely delivered Lucy to meet Bishop Norris—you can imagine why I was eager to ingratiate her and him. As to that business of her being a widow, no such a thing."

Avedon was glad to have a justified excuse to fly into a rage. "Now don't start that old scandal up again. She *is* a widow! I saw the papers myself."

"What you saw, if I'm not mistaken, are the papers announcing her brother Alex's death in Spain."

"Brother? But why would she mislead us about the relationship?"

"The intention was to pose as Alex's wife to ward off unwanted suitors—like you. But once she got a look at Tony's *beaux yeux,* she changed her mind and decided to enjoy the relative freedom of being a widow instead. There's a reason for it," he added, and explained about Mr. Pewter.

Avedon's shoulders slumped. "You mean to tell me she's rich, along with all the rest?" he asked despondently. His wealth was his last trump card.

"Rich as a nabob, not that it will do us much good. She don't really fancy Tony—or me. As to yourself—" He hunched his shoulders.

"If I'd had any idea, I never would have offered her a carte blanche," Avedon said earnestly.

"Carte blanche!" His companion's eyes goggled. "Now this she didn't tell me!" he said, eyes glistening avidly. "Do you know, Avedon, I begin to wonder if there isn't a spark of life in you after all. I had pretty well decided you were hopeless, but you force me to reassess your character. Today's spectacle, coming on top of a carte blanche, however . . . I fear you may have gone too far for even me to pull your chestnuts out of the fire, Cousin."

Avedon gritted his teeth. "You don't have to tell me. I was only temporarily insane. I still have the use of my wits."

The carriage drew up at the Rose. "Have you had lunch?" Morton asked.

"I don't know—er, no, I don't think so."

"Perhaps it's starvation that has turned you into a babbling idiot. Come along, I'll feed you. We must make plans."

As they entered the inn, Avedon said in a humble voice, "I would appreciate it if you don't tell Tony about—"

Morton patted his arm reassuringly. "Do you think I shall boast of being knocked down by you? Not likely, Cousin."

Tony did not return to the inn for another hour. He had met a chap from Oxford on High Street and had to give his rattler and prads a try.

"What is to be done?" Avedon asked. They sat in a private parlor, where Avedon toyed with his food and drank his wine. He had been brushed and washed and combed, to give at least an impression of respectability.

"Our best hope is that Norris doesn't recognize you when he goes to Chenely."

"We can't let him go there now!"

"Dear boy, do you really think Sally will let you prevent him from coming, when she wants that position for Rutledge? You might as well try to stop the wind. Make that a hurricane," he amended, as a picture of Lady Sara's determined face swam in his mind.

"I'll have to leave—go to visit one of my other estates till the bishop has left."

"That would give Lucy time to cool down, too." Carlton nodded.

"I have given up any hope of healing the breach there," Avedon said curtly.

"Of course you will see her and apologize before you leave."

"I shall write her a letter."

Carlton shook his head. "Pride, Cousin, is a wicked fault. You made a ridiculous spectacle of yourself. Swallow that ostrich egg in your throat and admit it—to Lucy. Tell her you are sorry. Tell her why you went darting off half-cocked."

As Avedon jerked at his collar, the old arrogance began peeping through. "It is true, I only went to Canterbury because I feared she was in danger. One cannot like to see a young lady jeopardize her reputation. . . ."

"Oh, I shouldn't tell her that, Avedon. I should tell her the truth, if I were you." He lifted his wine glass and smiled over the rim. "I liked you much better during these few hours when you unaccountably turned into a human being. I daresay Lucy would prefer that to a statue as well."

Avedon's first, instinctive response was to assume his haughtiest expression. Carlton watched with interest as the incipient sneer softened to a smile. "She is enough to melt ice, isn't she, Morton? Her eyes . . ."

Lucy stopped inside the front door of the Deanery and escaped her uncle by going to fetch her bonnet. She wanted a few moments to herself to collect her thoughts. She was mystified at Avedon's ghostlike appearance at the door, till she remembered his desperate question. "Are you married yet?" His voice was hoarse with anxiety and his eyes staring from his head. That was what had brought him pelting through the mud to Canterbury—concern that she had married Morton. That was what had turned him into a caveman and a raving lunatic. In theory she deplored such uncouth behavior, but when the cause was fear of losing her, she found it not only forgivable but gallant. Morton, the sly weasel, hadn't told the family that he was bringing her to meet Uncle Norris. Had he done it on purpose?

She wore a smiling face when she returned to the dining room. "Will you take me around the cathedral now, Uncle? I am very eager to see it. Such a pity Mrs. Percy is not here."

Yet she could not have repeated a word of its interesting history after the tour was over. She saw Avedon's glowering face in every leaded window and floating around the vaulted spaces of the clerestory. She was on pins to return to Rose Cottage for another round with him. The bishop droned on with the cathedral's history of burnings and rebuildings through the centuries, and Lucy said, "How horrid!" and "How interesting!" at what sounded like the proper times.

"And now we had best be on our way if we wish to arrive before dark," he said at last. "Mrs. Percy will be wondering what keeps us. I hope she isn't feeling poorly?"

"Not at all. She is on pins to see you."

"I'll just get my cases, and we'll be off."

Chapter Fifteen

Mrs. Percy, the real Mrs. Percy, now able to shine forth in all her widowed splendor, was curious at Lucy's state when she returned from Canterbury. Surely it was not just seeing her uncle again that put her in such a high state of fidgets. Her cheeks were as pink as peonies in full bloom. Her eyes held some secret glow, and her nerves were in tatters. She jumped like a grasshopper every time anyone spoke to her. She instituted no conversation of her own, and as often as not didn't even give a coherent reply to a direct question.

No interrogation could be instituted while they sat having dinner with the bishop. "We had a lamentable incident in Canterbury," Bishop Norris said, and told Mrs. Percy the story of the layabout who had attacked Mr. Carlton in front of the Deanery.

"That is shocking," Mrs. Percy exclaimed, but even that did not seem sufficient to account for

185

Lucy's trembling smile while Norris relayed the story.

After dinner the bishop retired to the study to read some literature picked up at the conference, and Mrs. Percy took the advantage of his absence to quiz Lucy.

"Lord Avedon stopped by this morning," she said in a tone of studied nonchalance. "Twice, actually. Higgs spoke to him the first time. The second time he came around to the garden, and I had a word with him."

Lucy smiled that dreamy smile. "What had he to say?" she asked politely.

"Not much. He just inquired when you had left. I daresay what he really wanted to know was when you would return. Perhaps he'll stop by this evening."

Lucy was coming to know him well enough to realize he would need more than a few hours to compose himself. "I shouldn't think so," she replied. "I told Morton not to call till tomorrow. Uncle will want an early night."

Was it Morton Carlton who had turned her into a moonling? "Call on the bishop?" she asked eagerly. "Do you mean he wished to speak to him about an offer?"

Lucy looked stunned at the suggestion. "Good gracious, no. There is nothing like that between us, Auntie. Morton is just a friend. A good friend," she added with another soft smile as she remembered his quick-wittedness in hustling Avedon from the scene of his disgrace.

186

As a last effort, though she knew it was no good, Mrs. Percy said, "Bigelow was with Avedon this morning."

That got a surprising response. "Was he? That's odd. I didn't see him at—" She came to an abrupt halt and blushed.

"At Canterbury?" Mrs. Percy prodded, trying to quell down her eagerness.

"Yes."

"You saw Avedon there?"

Lucy began a violent pleating of her skirt. "I believe Morton had a few words with him," she said evasively.

"Oh, really! Now what could have taken him to Canterbury? Odd he didn't mention to me that he was going."

Lucy looked up uncertainly. She was bursting to tell her exciting story to someone and said shyly, "The stupidest thing, Auntie. He took the notion we were seeing Uncle to get a special wedding license. He was quite upset."

"I see!" Light dawned, and Mrs. Percy moved her chair closer so that conversation could be carried on in the enjoyable conspiracy of whispers. "That bothered him, did it?" she said encouragingly.

Lucy fell into an unusual burst of giggles. "Oh, Auntie, it was so funny! He struck Morton, knocked him right down, and Uncle Norris came out waving his stick and threatening to call the constable."

"Dear me. That doesn't sound like Avedon!"

"No, and I fear he is so ashamed of himself that he will hesitate to call while Uncle is here."

Mrs. Percy nodded in complete understanding. "I've been working on our guest list for your uncle's dinner party while you were away. We really need Avedon to fill our table. Do you think a written invitation might draw him out?"

Lucy had been giving this problem some thought and said, "Lady Sara will make him come, for she very much wants the archdeacon's job for Dr. Rutledge. Morton told me. Perhaps if I wrote Avedon's card . . ."

"The very thing! What shall we say if Norris recognizes him?"

"I shouldn't think he will. I hardly recognized him myself. And if neither Morton nor I say anything, you know, Uncle will not suspect the truth."

The card was written that very night and delivered the next morning to Chenely, where it caused a monumental row.

"Not accept!" Lady Sara gasped, her eyes bulging from their sockets. "Not accept? You are mad, Adrian. Of course we shall accept."

"You must go, certainly," he agreed, "but I shall be busy."

"What can you possibly have to do that is of more importance than getting John his promotion?"

"I have to . . . to do my accounts," he said, bereft of inspiration.

"And polish your boots as well, no doubt. If you do not come with me, Avedon, I shall never forgive you. Never! You will never see me darken the door of Chenely again. We will be strangers from this day

188

forward. You know how long and hard I have worked for this promotion. If you scuttle it for me now, when I am this close—"

"If you have any hopes of landing that plum for Rutledge, the worst turn I could serve you is to show up at that party."

Lady Sara was completely bewildered. "What on earth are you talking about? He will be honored that you, an earl, go to see him. And we must have him here, too. I had thought tea, but as they are asking us to dinner, we shall make it a full, formal dinner. The Wedgwood, I think . . ."

"You can throw him a ball with my blessings, but don't expect me to attend."

"But *why*?" It was a cry from the heart.

"Because," he replied unhelpfully.

"That is not an answer, Avedon."

Avedon wavered on the edge of confessing all but found it too large a pill to swallow. "Don't ask, Sally. I just can't, and it would serve you ill if I did."

Lady Sara drew out her handkerchief and had recourse to a lady's last resort: tears. She sniffled angrily into the wisp of lace and linen, while pondering this mystery. Avedon paid no heed, and she sniffed more loudly. She saw with satisfaction that her tears were having the desired result and hiccuped roughly.

Avedon rose at once and went to comfort her. "Now, don't cry, Sal," he said. "You know I would help you if I could." A sob racked her whole body, while she peered hopefully up from the dry linen. She saw that while Avedon's heart was touched, his resolve remained firm. He put an arm around her shoulder, and she slid her head to his chest.

From this vantage point she considered the case. More than threats and tears were called for. Avedon was a good, ambitious brother who could not deny her his help without a strong reason. There was obviously something he was keeping from her, and she must draw it from him by fair means or foul. She sniffled forlornly and said, "We have always confided in each other, dear. There is no one I would sooner turn to than you in my time of need. Not even John is so understanding. I hope you would do the same if you were ever troubled." She rubbed her eyes to redness and turned them up to gaze soulfully at him.

"Of course," he said gently.

She lay her white fingers on his sleeve. "Lately, dear, I have sensed some ... withdrawal in you. Your strange behavior in jaunting off to Seaview the day before yesterday and returning so late. Then that bout with the bottle. And I heard from the servants that you did not drive your curricle home, but rode on an inn nag. Then, just yesterday, you were gone all day without a word to me. I was weak from worry." And still he did not confess.

"It was just business, Sal," he said, but with an appraising look.

He wanted to tell her, she was sure, but he was ashamed or afraid. The best way to ease his mind was to make him believe she overestimated his difficulty; then he could reassure her that it was not that desperate and tell her the truth. The worst catastrophe she could envisage was losing money. "I hope you have not been gambling, Adrian! Pray, don't tell me you have lost Chenely!"

"Good God, no. It has nothing to do with money. It is—a lady."

The worst he could do to a lady was not hard to figure out, though she knew Adrian would never do such a thing. Not to a *real* lady, at least. "Have you got someone in trouble?" she asked softly. No hint of censure tinged her dulcet voice.

"Sally! I think you know me better than that."

"But you said it is something that would give the bishop a disgust of you," she reminded him.

After her questions, broached in a completely sympathetic manner, Avedon began to see he was not quite the lowest form of humanity on the earth. "I daresay the bishop would think nothing of it, if he hadn't happened to witness it," he said and opened his budget.

Lady Sara resumed an upright posture and listened with the sharp ears of a judge. She said nothing while he poured out his heart. It was not till he finished his story—"So that is what happened"—that she gave tongue to her feelings.

"Have I got this quite straight, Avedon?" she asked in a frosty tone. "My brother engaged in a low, common brawl on no provocation whatsoever on the doorstep of Canterbury Cathedral, in front of Bishop Norris, whom you know perfectly well I have been trying to ingratiate for years? Does that about cover it, dear?"

"I told you my provocation!"

191

"Yes, that the bishop's niece went to meet him, accompanied by our cousin," she snapped. "And for *that* you have robbed John of his promotion. You have consigned me to living in a hovel the rest of my life! I shall be fortunate if John is not demoted to curate. I think you have taken leave of your senses." She rose and began pacing the room.

Avedon remembered that there was still one item he had neglected to confess. He hadn't mentioned the carte blanche, nor did he intend to do so now. "I thought they had run away to get married," he said.

"What if they had? She would still be family. Morton could have put in a word for John as well as you."

Avedon turned a disillusioned eye on her. "Well, by God, if that don't beat the devil. I have been pouring out my heart, and you don't care a tinker's curse for me. All you think of is yourself."

There was a long future of cadging off Adrian still to be enjoyed, and Lady Sara quickly recovered her wits. "Oh, my dear, it is you I am thinking of as much as anyone. You cannot blame me if I put my dear husband just a *tiny* bit before you. Now that you are deeply in love yourself with dear Lucy—and I could not be happier for you both—you know how the heart is touched. John will be so disappointed. We must think of some way out of this morass. Do you think Norris got a good look at you?"

"He looked straight at me."

"But you were wearing your hat?"

"I had on my lid, certainly."

"Then he only saw the bottom of your face. He must have been very upset, too, and he only saw you for a moment, all covered in dust. He will never recognize you. Wear your most elegant evening suit, and if you could adapt a different speech, a drawl perhaps."

"I can't drawl!"

"Of course you can, dear. You underestimate yourself." It was soon clear he also underestimated his sister. "And to put the clincher on it, I shall say you were here all day with me. If Norris notices any resemblance, he will think he is mistaken."

"Morton and Lucy know the truth."

"Morton won't tell. So thoughtful of him to try to help John by delivering Lucy to Canterbury and meeting the bishop, though the scoundrel ought to have let us know what was afoot. And Lucy won't tell, either, if you make her an offer."

"You're willing to lie to a bishop!"

"I have no intention of lying to him, dear. I shall just speak to Miss Percy when he happens to be listening in. In the unlikely case that Norris discovers any resemblance between you and the ruffian who assaulted Morton, we shall claim it was a cousin, who does happen to bear some family likeness. That will account for Morton's kindness in wishing to keep him out of the roundhouse. Now, let me see what must be done. I shall answer the dinner invitation, and you must dart down to Milhaven and rehearse Morton. And perhaps you should see Lucy, to propose to her," she added as an afterthought. "A widow will be doing pretty well to nab a title."

"She isn't a widow. Her chaperon is," he said, and had to explain all that intrigue to her.

"Well upon my word! The conniving little chit lied to us!"

"Yes, she is not much better than we are ourselves, when it comes down to it."

"*Better?* Oh, my dear."

Lady Sara gave a satirical little laugh and swanned out of the saloon to answer the dinner invitation. Avedon, his head in a swim, went to Milhaven to discuss the matter with Morton.

"The very thing. Leave it to Sal," Carlton said, smiling.

"We might possibly pull it off if Lucy went along with it, but—but I haven't the gall to suggest it," Avedon said. "And what if the bishop should recognize me before I get a chance to gain Lucy's help?"

"Yes, I see your problem. Let me go first. I told her I would call today. I'll get her aside and ask her assistance. Any other message you wish me to carry, Cousin?" he asked archly. "Never mind. I can probably do the job better without your help. Quite like Prissy and Tony. Some love affairs are best conducted with the lovers apart."

Avedon disliked to be left out of his own romance and came up with a different suggestion. "Bring Lucy here, if she's free. I would like to do my own explaining, Cousin."

"I'll try."

The bishop's visit brought a host of callers, and

Miss Percy was not free to abandon them, but she was encouraged that Avedon was making an effort at least to see her. She hid her joy as much as she could and said, "You may tell Lord Avedon that I will not reveal his identity to my uncle. If he can control his tongue and his fists for one evening, there is no reason he should not come. We would not have invited him if we had not thought him suitable to meet Bishop Norris."

"I'll give him your message," Mr. Carlton said, and returned to Milhaven to do it.

"How did she seem? Was she still angry?" Avedon inquired eagerly. He felt like a schoolboy with his first crush.

"Not angry, exactly. Just a little stiff. It will be for you to soften her with your persuasions. A tiara should go a long way."

"Lucy wouldn't be swayed by that."

"Of course not. She'd prefer a commoner. Odd she didn't tumble for me." Morton gave a knowing laugh and left.

Avedon returned to Chenely for more scheming with his sister as to what he should say to awaken Norris to the many excellencies of Dr. Rutledge. It was a long, exhausting day at both Chenely and Rose Cottage, but twilight came at last, and with the sinking of the sun, excitement rose in every heart except that of the bishop, and perhaps Lady Bigelow, who knew nothing of what was afoot and would not have cared if she had.

In all their harried planning, the conspirators overlooked one vital character. No one thought to inform Lord Bigelow what was afoot. In a moment of weakness Avedon had relented on the straw curricle, and Tony spent the day on the roads trying it out. As the hour for departure to Rose Cottage drew near, Mr. Carlton remembered and said, "It will be better if you don't mention having been in Canterbury yesterday, Tony."

"Eh? Why the deuce not?"

Carlton hesitated, disliking to make him privy to all that had happened. "Just don't mention it," he said. "The bishop would think you're a looney if he knew why you and Avedon were there. It will be better to say nothing."

"Adrian don't want to look stupid, you mean."

"Do *you*?"

Bigelow gave a sulking hunch, which his cousin took to mean he would keep his mouth shut, and they were off to Rose Cottage.

Chapter Sixteen

It was impossible to assemble any real elegance at Rose Cottage, but the ladies did what they could with the inferior equipment at hand. The centerpiece of roses arranged by Mrs. Percy's own hand was the prettiest thing on the dining table. For the rest of it the food would be fine, and there would be no shortage of it. Cook was preparing a turbot in white sauce, a roast of spring lamb, and a pair of capons, along with all the fresh vegetables that Lady Sara would sell her.

For the bishop's dinner party Lucy chose her green lutestring gown shot through with fine gold stripes, and with a darker green band around the waist. The small string of diamonds at her throat was unexceptionable, but it did not shine more brightly than her eyes. She sat in state with her aunt and uncle, awaiting the first knock of the front door. It was only the local vicar, Mr. Peoples, and his wife, come unfashionably early in their eagerness to meet the bishop. Next came the party from Milhaven, with Morton leading the way. Last to arrive were Lord Avedon and Lady Sara.

Avedon's eyes flew across the room to Lucy's. Her glance met his gaze for a fleeting moment, displaying neither pleasure nor pain but a studied indifference, before turning away. She rose to make the new arrivals known to her uncle.

"You know Lady Sara, of course," she said. "Deacon Rutledge's wife."

"We are bosom beaux." The bishop smiled and took her hand.

"My husband will be so sorry he missed you," Lady Sara simpered. "But you might as well try to make fish fly as to get him away from his work. He is the most dedicated man in the parish. But I don't have to tell you that, milord."

"No, indeed," he replied and turned his eyes to Avedon. He beheld a noble gentleman of impeccable grooming and beautiful if slightly stiff manners. It never so much as touched his mind that this stately lord had anything to do with a ruffian brawling in front of the cathedral. "Delighted to make your acquaintance at last, milord," the bishop said. "Your sister is forever singing your praises. She tells me you have some original Donne manuscripts in your library. I would give a monkey to see them."

"I will be happy to put them at your disposal at any time. I have been thinking I ought to give them to the Bodleian, for no one at home really appreciates them."

198

Lady Sara looked alarmed, whether through the danger of losing valuable documents or the insinuation that she did not live with her head in sermons, he was not sure. "Why, Adrian, John peruses them every chance he gets. Only he so seldom leaves the parish," she added dutifully.

"I'll drop by tomorrow, if that suits you?" the bishop suggested.

"You must come to lunch," Lady Sara said at once. "I have been waiting so long to show you all over my ancestral home, milord."

She slid onto the sofa beside the bishop and monopolized him while the others took up seats and accepted glasses of sherry. When the bishop took a glass, she said, "Perhaps just a tiny one, as this is such a special occasion." She lifted a glass, no less full than its fellows, and sipped daintily.

Lord Avedon quickly surveyed the room and went to sit near Lucy. Unfortunately Tony was hot at his heels. He looked warily around the room and said to his uncle in a stage whisper, "Morton says we ain't to mention Canterbury yesterday. Thought I might slip you the clue. We wouldn't want"—he tossed his head toward the bishop—"to know anything about it. Makes it look as if Lucy is a bit of a high flyer, you see."

Avedon gave a mental groan and thanked Divine Providence that Morton had thought to speak to Tony. "Right," he said, and continued to take up a chair beside Lucy.

As nine-tenths of the room was in on the conspiracy, they were left alone for a few moments, in hopes that the romance would come to the boil. "Lucy," he said in a low voice, "it was kind of you to invite me, after the way I behaved. You must have thought me mad. It was unforgivable of me."

She turned a sparkling eye on him. "I don't know what you are apologizing for, Lord Avedon." He smiled in relief. "Is it your calling me a liar, or a lightskirt, or is it only your beating Mr. Carlton at Canterbury? Surely you are not reverting to the tiling of your meadow? That is ancient history by now."

His spirits sank to hear his history recalled so vividly. "All of the above," he said, and fell silent.

Lucy rose briskly and went to sit with Lady Bigelow and Morton. When dinner was called, Lady Sara grabbed the bishop's arm and led the way to the table. Avedon offered his arm to Mrs. Percy. Lucy was not tardy to latch on to Morton, which left Tony to accompany his mother, and the vicar his wife. The conversation, led by Lady Sara, took an ecclesiastical turn over dinner. She inquired for news of the conference but showed no real interest in the archbishop's views on modernism in the church.

"I daresay the filling of our poor departed Dr. Nivens's shoes came up?" she asked artlessly.

"Not at the conference," the bishop told her. "That will be for the prime minister to decide."

She had often heard Avedon say the same thing but didn't believe a word of it. "But surely they will listen to your advice, milord," she said, and went on to drown him in butter. "You, so wise and experienced, will know better than anyone whom you wish to have working under you. The archdeacon must work closely with his bishop. Surely it is not just for the prime minister to say."

"There is a deal of politics mixed up in it," he told her. "And with our Tory government—" He hunched his shoulders. This was as good as saying John, an outspoken Whig, hadn't a chance.

Lady Sara gasped, and quickly filled her mouth with turbot, before it should betray her into some unladylike utterance.

Mr. Carlton adroitly turned the talk to other matters. In his haste he unthinkingly mentioned the visit to Canterbury. "I always seize every opportunity to take the tour," he said piously. "Personally, I find its architecture more interesting than St. Paul's. Certainly its history is."

"Yes, shocking how few people appreciate its history. Why, do you know," the bishop said, turning to include the entire table, "an ugly big fellow actually engaged Mr. Carlton in a fight there yesterday after lunch. Shocking. A great, uncouth lout he was, twice the size of Mr. Carlton. He looked as if he had been raised by wolves and acted it, too." A deadly hush descended over the table. "Shocking," he repeated again.

Into the silence Bigelow said, "By Jove, wouldn't I like to have seen that!" Carlton, sitting across from him, gave a killing stare. "If I'd been there, I mean, in Canterbury. Which, of course, I wasn't. And besides, I didn't go anywhere near the cathedral. Nor Avedon, either. We didn't go anywhere near it, did we, Uncle? I never left the High Street. Of our own village, that is to say. Heh, heh. Though now I think of it, Cousin,

201

it must have been just about the time you—you—"

"Avedon never left Chenely yesterday," Lady Sara stated firmly.

Lady Bigelow, who hadn't added a word to the conversation to that point, said, "Never left Chenely? I was sure I saw your mount at Milhaven early yesterday morning, Avedon."

"It was his groom," Lady Sara said. "Avedon's mount needed exercise, and as Adrian was unable to leave Chenely all day, I asked the groom to exercise it."

"A likely story!" Tony scoffed. "As if Avedon would let anyone get within a yard of his mount."

Mrs. Percy picked up the pickles and shoved them at Tony. "Do try these pickles, Tony," she said. At the same moment Morton said, "Would you mind passing the butter, Tony?" Bigelow stared from one to the other, taking the pickles, reaching for the butter. "Dash it, I only have two hands," he said. "And you need not all rush at me as if I was going to say something I shouldn't. I was only going to let on it was *your* mount Mama saw at Milhaven, Aunt Sally."

Lady Sara skewered him with a killing smile. "How could it be, when I never left Chenely all day, dear? I was home with Adrian, discussing new carpets for the village church."

The vicar looked up hopefully, but before he could urge on this scheme, the bishop intervened. Norris had already pegged Bigelow for a witless rattle and paid no heed to his ramblings. "I wouldn't mind more of those pickles," he said. "I haven't had any so good since my mama passed away."

"I'll give your cook the receipt," Lady Sara said swiftly, though they were not her pickles he was enjoying. "Better yet, you must take a few bottles home with you."

The conversation passed on to other matters, and the uneasy diners breathed a temporary sigh of relief. By sharp listening and fast talking and very little eating, a few other conversational perils were avoided, and eventually the hectic meal was finished without disaster. The ladies retired to the parlor, which was close enough to the dining room that they could hear the gentlemen's conversation without benefit of seeing them. Straining their ears toward the dining room left them very little time for conversation of their own. Lady Bigelow rested her head on a pillow and fell into a short doze.

After taking their port, the gentlemen joined the ladies. Lady Sara, who knew the bishop was a keen card player, suggested a hand of whist. "You will partner Mrs. Percy, Morton," she said, "and I shall partner the bishop." As the card table was being set up in the corner of the parlor, she said to Morton, "And make sure you don't win. We want him in a good mood."

"A good idea, but you aren't using all your wits, Sal," he replied. "Set up another table with the vicar and his wife against Tony and his mama, and you will leave Avedon free to pursue the heiress."

"Do you think I hadn't thought of that? Isabel doesn't play whist."

"Let 'em play Pope Joan, then."

Lady Bigelow was quite an adept at this childish

game. She overheard two of her favorite words and came to attention. "Pope Joan, did you say? Here, I have a deck in my reticule with the eight of diamonds already removed. Any number can play, so we will not have to leave two odd men sitting on the sidelines. Pope Joan, anyone?" She smiled invitingly at Avedon and Lucy.

Lucy saw the tentative smile on Avedon's face. She remembered all the iniquities she had suffered at his hands and was annoyed. Between him and Lady Sara, they had shamelessly turned this party into a vehicle to foster Dr. Rutledge's career. She and Mrs. Percy had gone along with it, helping them. And after all that he didn't even sit beside her when he came to the parlor. If Avedon thought he could now deliver his apologies quietly in a corner, where she must behave because of the audience, he was out in his reckoning. Oh, no, she would hear his apologies in complete privacy, and Lord Avedon would hear a few things about himself, too.

"Lovely, Lady Bigelow," she said, and rose to help set up another table. "I should be happy to play Pope Joan."

The look of shock on Avedon's face was well worth the ensuing hour of boredom. At nine-thirty the ladies had tea, the gentlemen had glasses of wine, and at ten the guests left.

The bishop expressed himself flattered at the attention of the noble guests. "I doubt Lady Sara would have been so charming if it were not for this appointment hanging fire," he said, laughing.

Lucy listened with interest. "What are Dr. Rutledge's chances, Uncle?" she asked.

"He and Collier are neck and neck. I personally prefer Rutledge, despite his wife, but of course Collier will get it. He has friends in the government."

"It doesn't seem right that a church appointment should hang on politics," Mrs. Percy said.

"They're hand in glove," he assured her.

The evening was only half over for the guests when they departed from Rose Cottage. Except for the vicar and his wife, the party repaired to Chenely to discuss the evening over a fresh pot of tea.

"That was a demmed dull scald, playing Pope Joan for pennies. We carried the thing off pretty slick, though," Tony congratulated himself. "The old boy never twigged to it that we thought Lucy had gone haring off with Morton. Mind you, I don't see that it would have made any difference if he had caught on. I mean to say, it's not as though we had done anything wrong. I do wish I had seen that row outside the cathedral. Who was it, Morton?"

"No one you know, Tony. A chap I met in London."

"Why was he beating you? Was it about horses, or money, or women?"

"Cards. And speaking of cards, Sal. You owe me three shillings. That is what I let Norris win from me."

Lady Sara never heard any conversation that was likely to cost her money. "I fear John's chances are very slim, with this business of a Tory government," she said to Avedon. "It seems so unfair."

"What you ought to do is make a stink about it," Tony said. "I mean to say, it ain't right, is it, the Tories giving all the plums to their own true blues? You'd think we was back in the days of Henry the Eighth, raping the monasteries."

"Watch your language, dear," his mother said. About the only meaningful word in the conversation for her was "rape."

"It still happens all the time," Lady Sara said sadly.

"Surely not around here!" Lady Bigelow exclaimed.

"We are speaking of nepotism, Isabel," Lady Sara explained.

Lady Bigelow shook her head in consternation. "What next?"

Lady Sara smiled her patient smile. "John was complaining before I left that Sir Alfred Harrison was made governor of some outlandish province in India over Mr. Seeton's head, when Seeton had more experience. But, of course, Seeton is a Whig, so his twenty years faithful service counted for nought. I was happy to see the *Times* made a fuss over the issue."

Avedon and Mr. Carlton exchanged a sharp, questioning look. "Indeed they did," Avedon said. "It was Pritchards who wrote the series of articles. He was at Christ Church with me."

Carlton said, "The idea can't come from us directly. We'll have to get someone else to approach Pritchards."

"And do it immediately, before the appointment is made," Avedon added.

There was excitement in the air. Lady Sara felt it before she quite figured out its cause. As sharp as a tack, she soon divined their meaning. "Cause a public ruckus in the press and the House, and shame the government into making a Whig appointment, you mean?" she asked.

"Exactly." Her brother smiled. "If we can get a few prestigious gents breathing flames down their necks, they won't dare hand another plum to one of their own."

"We'd better make a dart to London tomorrow and get working on it," Mr. Carlton said. He saw the quick frown that flitted across Avedon's face. "Lovemaking can wait, Cousin. A man may marry anytime, but if John doesn't get this appointment now, he will wait many a long year for another opportunity."

"He's right, dear," Lady Sara said urgently. "And meanwhile, I shall see that dear Lucy is kept safe for you."

"It won't take more than a day, two at the most," Avedon decided, and agreed to go to London.

"What are they talking about?" Lady Isabel asked her son. "If it is preventing all these horrid rapes, you ought to go with them, Tony."

"Of course I shall go," he said, throwing consternation into the rest of the group.

Chapter Seventeen

A note from Lady Sara was received early at Rose Cottage the next morning, reminding the bishop of his luncheon invitation to Chenely and inviting Lucy and Mrs. Percy to accompany him. As nothing was said of Avedon's having gone to London, Lucy was excited at the visit. Thus far the ladies had not gotten farther than the grounds of the estate at the garden party, and there was some eagerness to see the glories of the interior.

Bishop Norris was tempted out at an early hour by the lure of John Donne's manuscripts and drove over in his own carriage to spend the morning in the library, where he was so pestered by visits from a solicitous Lady Sara that he scarcely got to read a word. He did, however, enjoy not less than three cups of coffee, a plate of Cook's excellent macaroons, one of Avedon's specially imported cheroots, and a detailed account of the family's history, going back to its Norman roots.

His poor appetite at lunch was undoubtedly due to his morning's snacking, but Lady Sara had to wonder what accounted for Lucy's pecking at a better meal than she herself had served the night before. As Avedon was footing the bill, no expense was spared. She soon figured out the cause of Lucy's ill appetite and adopted a coy attitude after lunch, when Bishop Norris suggested she show the ladies the garden and let him get back to the manuscripts.

"You will be interested in this little knot garden, Miss Percy," she said. "It is the particular domain of the mistress of Chenely. It was planted eons ago by one of my ancestors." Lucy looked at a jumbled mass of herbs and small flowers, trying to find a pattern amidst the wilderness. "You can see the lack of the mistress's hand. Soon it will be back in form. Do you garden, Miss Percy?"

"I tended the garden at home after Mama died."

"Gardening is like walking. Once learned, it is never forgotten. You will have plenty to do here."

What Lady Sara really wanted to do was sit in the shade and order a glass of lemonade, but she spared no exertion in pursuit of John's promotion and soldiered bravely on through yew hedges and bowers of roses, misnaming five, according to Mrs. Percy's reckoning.

Mrs. Percy was a real gardener and enjoyed the tour. When at last the rest in the shade and the lemonade were forthcoming, it was Mrs. Percy who asked, "Where is Lord Avedon today, Lady Sara?"

"He had to help Morton with some business matter," she said vaguely.

"Gone to Hampshire, are they?"

"It may be necessary for them to take a quick jaunt to London as well. They tell me the banks there are easier to deal with."

"Hampshire and London! Then they will be gone for some little time, I expect."

"Oh, no! They will not be longer than two or three days. Adrian would not want to be away longer at this time," she said, smiling softly on Lucy. "I wouldn't be surprised if Adrian stops at the London residence and brings back a little something." Lucy adopted an expression of the utmost disinterest, but Mrs. Percy looked a question.

"The family engagement ring," Lady Sara said, nodding archly. "But we shan't discuss that. Only see how we have set Miss Percy—Lucy—to blushing. It is time we dropped formality. I want to call you Lucy a few times before I must begin calling you something else."

Lucy, already in a pelter at Avedon's leaving without saying a word to her, found this the last straw. "If you are implying that you will be calling me Lady Avedon, I must correct you. I have not had an offer from Lord Avedon," she said stiffly.

Lady Sara laid a white hand along her cheek to display chagrin. "Naughty me! I should not be revealing secrets. Not another word on that subject." Of course a good many more words were said before the party finally returned to Rose Cottage.

Time hung heavy for Lucy over the next days. She had hours in which to review all her past doings with Avedon, and found an insult at every bend. And on top of it all, he had apparently told his sister he was marrying her without even consulting her on the subject or taking a minute to drop her a note.

In London Avedon and Mr. Carlton were in a whirlwind of activity. Avedon opened his London residence and entertained a vast number of influential gentlemen, not omitting any Tory friends or connections. The subject of party nepotism arose at every meeting. Really it was close to a scandal, the shameless manner in which Liverpool showered perks on his friends. One hoped they would at least appoint a Whig archdeacon in the new vacancy that had arisen with Nivens's death, as Pritchards had recommended in the *Times*. Soon Mr. Wilson in the *Observer* and Mr. Parker in the *Morning Post* had taken up the same theme.

Mr. Carlton was not always present at these entertainments. He was on good terms with the Prince of Wales and endured an afternoon and evening of Prinny's company, during which he made known his views of this "appointment scandal" brewing in the press and lost fifty guineas at cards. Not a hope of ever getting it back from old Rutledge or Sal, either, but he might hit Avedon up for it.

Lord Bigelow was very little bother. He met up with an old school chum who had a sister summering with him. A dashed pretty chick, if a man didn't mind a good full figure, which Bigelow never minded in the least.

The campaign took a little longer than planned. Rutledge's appointment was not in the bag for four days. Avedon even made the sacrifice of spending two beautiful summer afternoons at Whitehall, listening to dull speeches. It was Lord Castlereagh who got him aside after a session to slip him the word. Gossip from such an unexceptionable source was taken as fact.

"About your brother-in-law, Avedon, you can ease up on the scandal-mongering. That matter is taken care of."

"*My* scandal-mongering?" Avedon asked, his brows lifted up to his hairline. "I can't imagine what you mean, sir." They both laughed. "Can I consider that positive?" Avedon asked. "I am eager to return to Chenely."

"It's not for me to say. I'm only a cabinet member, but I think you can go home with a light heart. Rutledge hounded you into this unusual summer visit to London, did he?"

"No, Lady Sara."

"Ah—of course. She is up to all the rigs. Give her my regards."

By leaving the next morning Avedon and Mr. Carlton reached home late in the afternoon. Bigelow left a little later. He invited his friends down to Milhaven for a few days, and you couldn't ask a lady to set out at first light.

At Chenely Lady Sara took one look at her brother's smiling face and threw herself on his chest.

212

"Adrian, you have done it! You are the best brother in the world."

"Morton was a great help. Prinny bit his ear to the tune of fifty guineas. Cheap at the price."

Lady Sara blissfully ignored this talk of guineas and said, "I have not been idle while you were away, dear. You will find a certain young lady on thorns, waiting for you to call."

"You've seen Lucy?" he asked eagerly.

"Oh, my dear, seen her! We have virtually lived in each other's pockets. I like her tremendously. She is not one of those bold, forthcoming chits, and even if the family is only genteel, she has such a good fortune. Sixty thousand, I learned from Norris. Not many noble ladies bring that sort of blunt with them—and an uncle who is John's bishop."

"Lucy is expecting me to call?"

"You have time to speak to her before dinner, if you move quickly. You'd best wash up and put on a clean shirt."

"And my best jacket." Avedon laughed, already darting for the stairs.

Lady Sara made a run to the pantry to select a ham and have it placed in her carriage, for she would leave tomorrow early to take the news home to John, before he heard it through official channels.

Lucy, loitering near the parlor window that gave her a view of the road, saw a yellow curricle dashing toward Rose Cottage. It's reckless pace led her to believe Tony was holding the ribbons, and her heartbeats did not accelerate unduly. His coming, however, suggested that Avedon, too, might be home. Naturally *he* did not come galloping to see her.

The curricle made a wild, reckless turn into the entrance to Rose Cottage. Tony was going to fall right into the ditch if he didn't slow down. Lucy mentally prepared a lecture for him. As the curricle drew closer, she saw that the head and shoulders belonged not to Bigelow but to his uncle. She gasped and fled from the window. She had no intention of being caught in such flagrant spying. When Higgs admitted the caller, she sat leafing desultorily through the latest issue of *La Belle Assemblée*.

She looked up with every evidence of disinterest when Avedon was announced. "Oh, you are back," she said. "We did not expect you so soon. Lady Sara mentioned you might have to go to London as well. I hope your meetings were successful."

He advanced into the room, smiling warmly. "Entirely successful."

"Good." She reached for the bell cord. "I shall ask Higgs to bring us some wine, and call Mrs. Percy." But she didn't do it. Her hand hovered on the cord, not moving it an inch.

"No!" he exclaimed, and hurried forward. Lucy assumed a haughty expression. "You can have nothing to say to me that my chaperon might not hear, Avedon." Her hand remained motionless.

Avedon took it and removed it from the cord, then closed his fingers firmly over it. "You're right, of course. This time I mean to do the thing properly. The bishop himself would find nothing to object to." His voice was warm, and his eyes were hot. He took her other hand, drew her to her feet, and proceeded toward the door.

Lucy thought he meant to go in search of her aunt, and was furious with him. He closed the door, and turned back to her. "I don't think we want Higgs listening, however," he said.

There was a crackling feeling of tension in the air and a very determined light in Avedon's eyes. Lucy lifted her chin and said, "What is this great secret we must keep from Higgs?"

"That I have subverted the entire government. Rutledge is going to be the archdeacon," he announced.

"Avedon! Is that all you have to say?" she exclaimed angrily. "Is that why you left? To sneak around, scheming to get a job for your brother-in-law?"

"We don't want Sal around our necks when you come to Chenely."

"Why should I be going to Chenely?" she asked, with studied obtuseness.

Avedon looked around the little parlor. "Because I don't think we would be happy here, and you have already sold Fernbank."

A flush crept up her neck and tinged her cheeks to rose. "I don't know what you are talking about."

"I think you do."

"I made the error of mistaking you for a gentleman on former occasions," she reminded him. "This time I shan't have to walk home at least."

"You didn't walk the last time. You stole my curricle."

"It served you right! How dare you come here without even apologizing! And telling Lady Sara I would weed the knot garden," she charged.

"Knot garden?" He frowned. "We'll forget that non sequitur for the time being. I confess I have behaved abominably, Lucy, and so have you. Had you not led us to believe you were a widow, none of those things would have happened—the arguments, the carte blanche, the tiling of the meadow."

"The ultimatum regarding the garden party, the brawl at the cathedral," she added helpfully.

"Really quite a litany of my sins you have prepared. And I used to be considered a very proper gentleman."

"Well, you aren't! You're a proud, conceited, arrogant—lecher!"

"And you have been, within the space of two weeks, a war wife, a widow, a runaway bride—"

"And a victim," she added.

He smiled at her temper tantrum. "There's only one thing left for you to be."

"A corpse, I suppose."

"Eventually, but meanwhile, it was my fiancée I had in mind."

"You sound as if I have been everyone else's."

He drew her into his arms and gazed at her upturned face. He watched, entranced, as she tried to stop her lips from trembling by pulling the lower one between her teeth. "I don't give a damn if you have. You're mine now," he said, and lowered his head to claim his prize.

Lucy's lower lip eased free and was crushed

216

against the assault of his embrace. Her frustrations melted into acceptance as the kiss continued. No memory of Ronald Pewter marred the sublimity of that kiss. It was enhanced by a foretaste of pleasure to come. When he released her, she looked dazed.

"You might have asked me first," she said, pouting.

"I was afraid you'd say no, for spite."

"I'm not talking about that kiss. I mean, to be your wife."

Avedon lifted her hands and kissed her knuckles. "You have to marry me now. You've spoiled me for anyone else. What would I want with some prim and proper bride, when I have gotten accustomed to a delightful baggage like you? I love you so much, I turned into a raving madman when I thought you and Morton—"

The last vestige of opposition dissolved at his earnest declaration. "Oh, Adrian." She laughed. "How can you be so foolish? I only went to show you a lesson. I have been wanting to give you one ever since you cut up so stiff at me in the village, before you even knew me."

"I knew even then you were going to be trouble. Too pretty by half. Perhaps I was already a little jealous of Tony."

"Only a little?" she asked with a smile.

"Yes, I saved my major fit for Morton. A lucky thing your uncle didn't recognize me. Shall we tell him the news?"

"Oh, yes. He will want to perform the ceremony."

"So will Archdeacon Rutledge," Avedon said, with a leery look, and went to the door.

"You mean Lady Sara will want him to."

"If worse comes to worst, we can always elope," Avedon decided. "A dash to Gretna Green, an elegant match over the anvil ... All the crack." He turned a startled face to Lucy. "Good Lord!"

"Don't look at *me* like that. It was *your* idea."

"That's what amazes me," he said, and laughed in surprise. "And what amazes me even more, I *meant* it. You've depraved me, Lucy Percy. How can I ever thank you?"

Certainly Higgs, peering in through the keyhole, thought them both past reclaiming. And with a bishop in the house, too!

Mrs. _____ nodded in complete understanding. I've been working on _____ _____ _____ uncle's